TO THE ISLANDS

TO THE ISLANDS

★ A NOVEL BY ★
RANDOLPH STOW

Taplinger Publishing Company/New York

Revised edition first published in
the United States in 1982 by
TAPLINGER PUBLISHING CO., INC.
New York, New York   C . I

Copyright © 1958, 1982 by Julian Randolph Stow

Library of Congress Cataloging in Publication Data
Stow, Randolph, 1935–
    To the islands.
    I. Title.
PR9619.3.S84T6   1982   823   81-21407
ISBN 0-8008-7739-X   AACR2

To
SALLY GARE AND BILL JAMISON
with admiration

My cell 'tis, lady, where instead of masks,
Music, tilts, tourneys and such courtlike shows,
The hollow murmur of the checkless winds
Shall groan again; whilst the unquiet sea
Shakes the whole rock with foamy battery.
There usherless the air comes in and out:
The rheumy vault will force your eyes to weep,
Whilst you behold true desolation.
A rocky barrenness shall pierce your eyes,
Where all at once one reaches where he stands,
With brows the roof, both walls with both his hands.

Marston: *The Malcontent*

Still islands, islands, islands. After leaving Cape
Bougainville we passed at least 500, of every shape,
size, and appearance.... Infinitely varied as these
islands are — wild and picturesque, grand sometimes
almost to sublimity — there is about them all an air
of dreariness and gloom. No sign of life appears on
their surface; scarcely even a sea bird hovers on their
shores. They seem abandoned by Nature to complete and
everlasting desolation.

Jefferson Stow: *Voyage of the Forlorn Hope*, 1865

PREFACE TO THE REVISED EDITION

To The Islands was first published in 1958, and completed not long after I had passed my twenty-second birthday. Understandably, it contains many faults, due partly to immaturity, but more to the fact that my technical competence was not equal to my ambition, which in retrospect makes me realise how horizons narrow in middle age. In reissuing it in this very slightly abridged version, I am conscious that it still asks for the tolerance which most reviewers were kind enough to show when it was new, on the grounds that its author (who no longer seems to be myself) was too young to know his own limitations. Nowadays I should hardly dare to tackle such a *King Lear*-like theme; but I do not regret having raised the large questions asked here, and so wisely left unanswered. If the novel retains any interest, other than as an historical-sociological document, it may be because this story of an old man is really about a certain stage in the life of a sort of young man who has always been with us, and always will be.

In the original edition I was consciously making propaganda on behalf of Christian mission-stations for Aborigines, in particular for one Mission on which I had worked for a short time, and which seemed in danger of closing down. Australian writers before me had generally given missions and missionaries a bad press, and in earlier days some had deserved their low opinion. By 1957, however, the year in which the novel is set, it seemed to me that at least one of them was performing a valuable service to the Aboriginal community which it housed and employed, and which, indeed, it could be said to have created. Though the Government contributed largely to the lodging and education of children, medical services and the rations given to "indigents" (nomads), it could not easily have distributed its charity without the facilities provided by the Church of England and its servants, employed at merely token salaries. It was clear that if the Church felt forced to withdraw its backing from that isolated village, one of only two settlements in a region about the size of Tasmania, the effect on the inhabitants would be disastrous.

For that reason there was in the novel a good deal of talk by the white characters about their difficulties and hopes, and even a very tepid love-interest, introduced not for its own sake but to suggest that at least two Europeans would remain committed to the Mission. Most of those passages have gone now, as the cause was lost long ago. The book did get itself mentioned in the Federal Parliament ("A brilliant story", said

Hansard), but that was in connection with the alleged need for Professors of Australian Literature. Chairs were duly invented for them; and the Mission, in the late 1960s, was abandoned.

Even though I saw for myself the financial problems which confronted the Church of England there, this withdrawal strikes me as astonishingly irresponsible. The Aborigines were removed, willy-nilly, from the "country" to which they were so deeply attached (as who would not be, for it is stunningly and majestically beautiful), and sent to live near the town of Wyndham. The result was exactly what could have been predicted: drink, prostitution, violence and gaol.

In the early 1970s a combination of white men and Aborigines managed to secure a quite substantial Government grant and went back to the Mission lands. One of those involved was my friend Daniel Evans, who is quoted extensively in Chapter 2, and who was (there seems no harm in revealing) the original of Justin. In 1974 I heard some very painful accounts of this deracinated, replanted community. Alcohol, which was never known there in the Church of England's time, was periodically taking hold of the entire population; there was violence, especially the beating-up of women by men, and the intimidation of strangers; and a visiting film-maker reported having had a conversation, at 10 a.m., with three girls of eleven or twelve who were rolling drunk, and told him about their careers as prostitutes.

I have heard no further reports, and sincerely hope that these were teething-troubles, and that the people have returned to something like their former life-style. Alcohol is certainly a great problem, and one which did not arise in the 1950s, when Aborigines had few if any civil rights and were forbidden to drink. But it need not be a problem forever. In New Mexico and Alaska I have visited Indian and Eskimo communities which were "dry" by their own choice, and the extreme isolation of the former Mission would make such voluntary prohibition very effective.

The hostility shown by some of those people to white visitors, as reported to me in 1974, may prove a worse problem. In 1957 disagreements and even flaming rows between black and white were not unknown, but it was generally perceived that both races were necessary for the continuation of a community which all wished well. Even the Umbali massacre of 1926, described in Daniel's words in Chapter 2, had had one positive effect on race-relations: the courage and intransigence of "Djadja" (Father) Gribble, the then Superintendent, had left, it seemed to me, a sharper memory than the atrocities of the murdering policemen. Some of the children rescued then are probably still alive. One wonders what their feelings are now, after having been abandoned by their Church and exiled to a township not noted for enlightened attitudes on racial matters. I fear that the often affectionate relations between black and white which I was lucky enough to see in that place may not be seen there again, at least for a generation or two.

I began my Note to the original edition with the curt statement: "This is not, by intention, a realistic novel", which has been misinterpreted as a sort of manifesto. In fact, it merely expressed my irritation with the tyranny, in Australia, of social realism. In the 1950s novelists, one gathered, were supposed to concern themselves with Statistically Average Man, and he did not interest me. But in other respects I aimed, as I always have, at the most precise description I could achieve of things I had experienced with my own senses. Except in the choice of subject-matter, I have always been a fanatical realist.

The return to literature of Patrick White, after a long silence, soon made it superfluous to attack social realism in Australia. But this also led to a misapprehension about *To The Islands*, which many academics (who have rather innocent ideas about the speed with which writers and printers work) took to have been written under the influence of *Voss*. In fact, it was in the publishers' hands before *Voss* was available in Australia, and had been begun much earlier. Literary influences there certainly were, and the text confesses them — "The Lyke-Wake Dirge", *Everyman*, *King Lear* — but they had been assimilated over some years.

Though I covered on foot a great deal of the dramatic country forming the Mission's territory, my work as ration-storeman prevented me from making any very long journey. But I did, in writing of Heriot's travels, consult the accounts of several explorers of the North Kimberley, particularly C. Price Conigrave's book *Walkabout* (Dent, 1938), and realised that I had, in effect, seen all the landscapes Heriot would have encountered. At the time I was rather haunted by a passage written by a sea-explorer of that region, a brother of my great-grandfather's; and as it was much in my mind, I have added it to this edition as an epigraph.

Daniel Evans told me much about the language and mythology of his people, and on both subjects I received further enlightenment from the work, published and unpublished, of the linguist Dr A. Capell. His manuscript notes on the language were of great assistance in my dealings, as ration-storeman, with the nomadic Aborigines. I later became, for a short time, a student of his at the University of Sydney.

The lines by Gerard Manley Hopkins on page 10 are reprinted from his *Poems* by kind permission of the Oxford University Press.

TO THE ISLANDS

Tired and embittered missionary to
Australian aborigine colony flees into
the outback to die, accompanied by
aborigine friend.

I

A child dragged a stick along the corrugated-iron wall of a hut, and Heriot woke. His eyes, not yet broken to the light, rested on the mud-brick beside his bed, drifted slowly upwards to the grass-thatched roof. From a rafter an organ-grinder lizard peered sidelong over its pulsing throat.

Oppressed by its thatch, the hot square room had a mustiness of the tropics. On the shelves of the rough bookcase Heriot's learning was mouldering away, in Oxford Books of this and that, and old-fashioned dictionaries, all showing more or less the visitations of insects and mildew.

Collecting himself from sleep, returning to his life, he said to the lizard: 'The sixty-seventh year of my age. *Rien n'égale en longueur les boiteuses journées* —'

Outside, the crows had begun their restless crying over the settlement, tearing at his nerves. The women were coming up to the kitchen. He could hear their laughing, their rich beautiful voices. Already the heat was pressing down on him, the sheet under him clung to the skin of his back, and it not yet six o'clock and a long day.

'When shall I be cool?' demanded Heriot of the lizard. 'Soon the weather must change, the Wet is over, an old man can begin to live again.' He tore aside further his sagging mosquito net, and the lizard took fright, dropped down, scurried to the doorway and froze there, waving a frantic paw.

Heriot sat up and lowered his feet to the floor, slow in all his movements under the weight of his years and tiredness. Walking to the shower, his feet brushed the ground, his head was bent and his eyes lowered from the wounding light. Yet he was a tall man, stooping there under the overhanging thatch, a big man with his wild white hair, his face carved and calm. The lizards scattered from his path, the crows cried. Under running water, coursing the furrows of his face, a little of his weariness was washed away.

Deep in fading grass the country stretched away from the hut, between the rocky ridge and the far blue ranges, dotted with white gums, yellow flowering green-trees, baobabs still clinging to their foliage. And from the grass, which harboured also goats, creepers and all rustling reptiles, rose the Mission, the ramshackle hamlet of huts and houses, iron and mud-brick and thatch, quiet below the quiet sky.

So still, so still in the early heat. Standing at the door of the shower, pulling on his shirt, he watched Mabel walking through the grass, Djimbulangari slowly following. They moved as he did, loosely and tiredly, two old women with their hair tied in kerchiefs, their dresses hanging straight on their thin bodies. Looking at Mabel he thought that he had never seen her in any clothes but these, the dirty coloured skirt sewn to a flourbag bodice on which the mill brand was still bright green and legible. Picking their way like cranes through the grass, talking occasionally, not looking at one another. Old, dried-out women, useless and unwanted.

The guitar began behind one of the huts, plunk, plunk, plunk, while he was shaving, and he accompanied it with his mumbled singing:

> 'There was a little nigger
> And he couldn't grow no bigger
> So they put him in a Wild West show —'

The boy Arthur passed outside, straight and springy, absurd in the vanity of his youth. Sitting in the dust beneath a baobab an ancient man, Garang, with grass caught in his long and filthy hair, watched him expressionlessly.

'You know, Garang,' Heriot reflected, 'and I know, how short a time this game can be played. Soon no girls will look when he goes past, soon the girls themselves will be black and dry as Djediben. Blessed,' said Heriot to his face in the shaving mirror, 'are the arrogant, for they have the gift of innocence.'

He smiled at himself in the mirror. But it was wrong, the muscles of his face were stiff, and the twist of his mouth was no smile. How long, thought Heriot, covering his mistake with lather, it must be since I have laughed.

And the mirror was broken, the wooden shutter of the window broken. Broken, broken. He saw himself as a great red cliff, rising from the rocks of his own ruin. I am an old man, an old man. *J'ai plus de souvenirs que si j'avais mille ans.* And this cursed Baudelaire whining in his head like a mosquito, preaching despair. How does a man grow old who has made no investment in the future, without wife or child, without refuge for his heart beyond the work that becomes too much for him?

Because his despair grew on the cracked face in the cracked glass he turned away and finished dressing. And hurried then — because it was six o'clock and Harris was coming out to ring the rising bell — to the office to tune in the wireless to the morning schedule.

'...Listen to medical calls,' said the voice, and the bell rang, clamorous and prolonged, under the baobab outside.

Then the early-morning static, and a woman's voice, far away and unintelligible. Heriot, seated beside the set with a pad in front of him, sketched a crumbling cliff with the profile of the Sphinx.

'. . . Lie up a few more days,' said the voice. 'Get him to take it easy. And keep in touch, let's know how he's getting on. All right?'

'Righto, thanks, Tom,' said the woman in the static.

'That's the lot,' said the voice. 'I'll read the traffic list. I have traffic on hand for —' But the static caught him as he read the call signs. Heriot, twiddling with the controls, listened for Don L, but there was nothing. Only further away, through worse static, another voice began: 'D J, D J, D J, good morning, Tom.'

'Nothing,' Heriot said. 'Nothing.' He crumpled the paper with the drawing in his fist and threw it away, and turned off the wireless, and sat there for a moment, his chin in his hands. Then his eyes fell on the mailbag inside the door, reminding him that in the night, while he had lain quiet in a sleep of sedatives, the boat had come back with communications from the other world.

Kneeling by the bag he ran his old hands, darkly blotched on the backs, steadily through the pile of letters, searching for the envelope with his typewritten name, his freedom. But when he found it and had torn it open and read the short message, every part of him went suddenly still, his mouth was still, only the room and the crows and the late, pestering mosquitoes seemed to echo: 'Nothing.'

Before Bob Gunn's path a snake whisked its black length into the grass.

'*Ali!*' shouted the children outside the church. '*Ali, lu!* Brother bin see *wala*!'

'Go away,' Gunn told them as they gathered round him. '*Bui!*'

'*Ali!*' cried the girls, seized with laughter. 'He say *bui*! Brother talk language.'

'You look out,' Gunn said. 'Might be cheeky feller, that one.' But they were all round the grass, and the snake somewhere in the middle. He poked cautiously in the thick growth between himself and the bare brown feet of the girls poised for flight at the edge.

Ruth had a stone in her hand, Amazonian, her big white teeth showing. '*Ali!*' she shouted, 'there, look.' The line of girls dispersed, screaming, as she threw the rock. For a moment the shining snake appeared, then vanished with a flick into the freedom of the denser grass.

'He take off, all right,' Ruth said. 'He no monkey, that one.' And the girls, always ready to laugh, giggled and cried: '*Ali!*' around and behind her.

'Well, we lost him,' Gunn said. '*Mire badi*, never mind.' He abandoned his stick and walked away, while behind him they screamed to one another: 'He say *mire badi*! Brother talk language.'

Behind the church, in his cassock, smoking a last cigarette before the service, Father Way gazed absently at the new sun overhanging the distant blue hills. He looked round as Gunn came up. 'One thing you have to give this country, it's colourful. Look at those hills, like a bad watercolour.'

3

'The trees are greener up here, too,' Gunn said. 'Leaf-green. Trees down south are going to look pretty drab after this.'

'And the cliff — see that.' Together they looked at the high cliff across the river and found it burning red with the morning light, rising above the bright green of gums and mangroves and baobabs on its banks. 'Now, and at sunset,' Way said, 'you can see that for miles.'

Gunn had rolled a cigarette and was squatting on one heel. 'Just missed a black snake,' he said. 'The girls scared it. They like their *wala* hunts.'

'We've got everything,' Way said. 'Everything you could possibly wish elsewhere.'

'These crows — twice as big and loud as any civilized crow.'

'And the damn cockatoos. They tore up my peanuts and ate them. I thought I was going to do something for the agriculture of the Kimberleys.'

Gunn said, looking across at the cliff: 'By the time this country's ready for agriculture the rest of the world will have blown away in fine dust.'

'Things are working out,' Way said, 'I think. There are plans for opening up more country, running some more cattle. Not,' he admitted, 'that I'm any less concerned, but I'm more optimistic. Once Heriot's affairs are fixed up and the new man comes we won't feel so uncertain about everything.'

'Did the council find a new man?'

'They said in their last letter they had two candidates.'

'The mail came last night. Mr Heriot probably knows by now.'

'It'll be a relief,' Way said. 'To him as much as to anyone. He's too old.'

'Harry's older.'

'But more stable. Less to worry about.'

Picking at the grass, Gunn said slowly: 'I wonder whether, when he's dead, people won't think again about Mr Heriot.'

'I'm a charitable sort of bloke,' Way said with a faint smile, 'as a clergyman. I'll just say I prefer people who have a certain warmth about them. Especially on missions.'

'He's one of the old school, though. It was tough for them, they didn't have time for warmth. And he has achieved something, you can't take that from him. I don't see how we can sit in judgement on him, now, when it's so much easier.'

Way said dryly: 'You're young, Bob, you make me ashamed of being so old and inflexible. But I stick to this: a man who goes round spreading civilization with a stock-whip gets no admiration from me.'

Gunn, staring at the ground, pulled out his tin to roll another cigarette.

'No time for that,' Way said. 'I'm two minutes late already. My wife

has a trying time waiting at the organ with the girls whispering, "*Ali,
Mana wipe her nose, Mana scratch her neck*," all round the church.'

'I'd better take off,' Gunn said. He got up and walked round by the
grass half-walls to the open front of the iron church where the men stood
waiting under a baobab.

Murmuring: 'Good day, brother.'

'*Nandaba grambun, abula?*'

'You talk language, brother?'

'*Jau,*' Gunn said. 'Little bit.'

'Good day, *abula.*'

Good day, Michael; good day, Justin; good day, Edgar; good day,
Richard; good day to all my brethren.

Kneeling on the ant-bed floor, rock-hard under her knees even through
the thin hassock, Helen Bond watched Heriot at his rigid prayers near
the front of the church.

Thinking: What does he say, morning after morning, kneeling up so
straightly? How does he go on, with always the same day ahead? Is it the
prayer itself that gives him strength?

He had raised his head now, his neck was darkly burned below the
white hair. His mind is somewhere else, Helen thought. What does he
think about, what has he been thinking to himself for all these years and
years?

From a rafter above his head a lizard dropped to the floor, stood in the
aisle waving one forepaw. She, watching it, became aware of a sort of
rustle of attention among the people, and found that they too were
watching, with the amusement and the tenderness they kept for the
eccentricities of wild life. But Heriot had not noticed, his eyes were fixed
on a distant tree showing over the half-wall of the church, and his body
still had that tensity of concentration that belonged to his prayers, so that
she felt suddenly ashamed that she could be so easily distracted, and
covered her eyes with her hands. But could think of no prayer, having
already said everything that seemed necessary.

Afterwards, standing outside with Gunn, she watched Heriot walk
stiffly back to his office, and said: 'I don't know what's the matter with
him. He let me examine him, and he seemed to be in wonderful condition
for a man of his age. Yet sometimes he seems too tired even to say "Good
morning".'

'Terry thinks he's going troppo.'

'Troppo?'

'It's not in the *Nurse's Encyclopedia.* Means going queer from being
too long in the tropics. — Do you remember, in the war, the cartoons
about going troppo and drinking jungle juice?'

At the end of the road, where the trees met, 'There's Djediben in her
new dress,' said Helen. 'She looks ready for a garden party.'

Gunn laughed. 'Gosh, what a figure. She could be sixteen.' They watched the slim, middle-aged woman advance down the road in her almost fashionable dress. Her body with its long lines had the grace of a girl's, she walked delicately on her gross bare feet.

'*Ali!* real pretty fellow now,' Helen called to her.

The small black face split open with a screech of laughter. 'You pretty fella, sister, yeah, you.'

'No, you, Djediben.'

'*Ali,* sister!' screeched Djediben, convulsed with laughter, and came and embraced her with thin black arms, touching gently with her palms Helen's breasts and shoulders, circling her waist with a spider arm. 'Sister,' she sighed lovingly, hiding her face against Helen's neck.

'You old smoodger,' Helen said.

Gunn asked: 'Where's Dambena, Djediben? Still camping in the bush?'

'Eh, Nambal — that way.'

'He likes the bush, eh?'

'*Jau,* 'im like 'im budj.'

'You'd better go and see him. He'll be getting off with another old woman pretty soon.'

'*Jau,*' screamed Djediben, ''nother old woman. Brother.'

As she stifled her amusement against Helen's neck a wad of chewed tobacco dropped from behind her ear and fell in the dust. With a wail she fell on her knees to search for it and having found it sat crouched in grief over her thin hand. '*Worai, worai,*' she lamented, rocking slowly with desolation. '*Mundju* all binidj!'

'It's only dusty,' Helen said consolingly over the keening, 'and this is ration day, you'll get more this afternoon.'

'Aaaah,' crooned Djediben.

'*Mire badi,*' Gunn said. 'Never mind.'

Suddenly, as if a tap had been turned off, all lamentation ceased. The woman got to her feet, put the tobacco in her mouth, and walked silently away.

'Funny old thing,' Helen said. 'So many moods in one little woman. It's a wonder she didn't stay. She must have known if she kept wailing long enough I'd give her a cigarette to chew.'

'Eldritch is the only word for Djediben.'

'That sounds a bit sinister.'

'She is, I think. Intelligent and inscrutable. Lots of dark depths under the smooth manner.'

'She's Rex's mother. You know, the famous Rex.'

'Rex's mother?' Gunn asked sharply. 'I didn't know that.'

'I found it in an old file. It might explain some things about Rex.'

Looking along the baobab avenue to where, in the shade-stippled dust,

Djediben had sat herself down, Gunn said slowly: 'I'm feeling a bit worried.'

'About what?'

'Rex.'

'What has he done now?'

'He's come back.'

Helen turned her head and stared, so that the light, falling through the leaves, filled her eyes and the clear, honey-coloured depths of them. 'Here?'

'Here.'

'But how?'

'Well, Stephen was coming back, that was all arranged, and somehow Rex got hold of him and persuaded him to introduce him to Terry. And of course Terry didn't know anything about Rex, and finished up by bringing him back in the boat last night.'

'Oh, Lord. What will Mr Heriot do?'

'I can't think. But he can't blame Terry — I mean, it was his first trip, and he says no one told him about picking up stray passengers. It was just his lousy luck that it had to be Rex.'

'But I can't understand why Rex should want to come back, not after everything that happened before. He knows what Mr Heriot thinks of him.'

'I think it's just that he scores off the white man by being here at all. Especially off Terry.'

'Poor Terry,' Helen murmured.

There was a kind of amusement in her voice, not for the first time when speaking to Gunn of Dixon. Oddly, Gunn found himself resenting it, on behalf of the older man, whose simplicity made him feel fraternal.

Behind her the altar cross and candlesticks glinted in the shadowy sanctuary. She was pretty; but at times so intensely serious that he found himself withdrawing a little. He could guess that she had been used to success, her schooldays probably a litter of trophies, so that her one failure, as a medical student, had hit her hard. And now, as a mission nurse on a salary of sixty pounds a year, she was determined not to fail again. She was perhaps a fanatic of sorts, like a nun.

'You're looking tired,' she said.

'I was up in the middle of the night,' he said, 'to meet the boat and unload.'

'You have a hand in everything,' she said. 'There's no need for you to do so much work, all you need do is run the school.'

'How can you not get involved?' he said. 'It grows on you.'

Sent there by the Education Department, to stay a year or two, he had never intended to be involved. But the country had taken him in. There was first of all the easy affection of the children, brought up to expect from an adult nothing else but affection. And from them his feeling had extended to their parents and older siblings, the bush nomads, the rock and waters of the land itself. The phrase '*gre ngaianangga*, my country', so often in their mouths, would keep recurring to his mind.

At times he chafed at his life there, the goldfish-bowl existence of a white man. It would be good, he thought on empty nights, to get drunk with a friend like Terry Dixon, to flirt, or something more, with a girl like Helen. But there was around them that fence of vocation. And he was being drawn within it. The country and Heriot, between them, were taking possession of him like a colony.

Her hair would be soft to touch. He would have liked to cup his hands around her face.

One night he dreamed that Heriot was making magic on him. And he woke rebelling. I'm too young, he was telling Heriot. I want to fool around, live the life that Terry has given up, away from blackboards and from church.

At the camp the barking of many dogs commented on some arrival or departure. A child shouted at the far end of the village. He looked at the white goats deep in pasture, beyond them the encircling blue of the hills.

'Look at Djediben,' Helen remarked. 'Asleep again.'

He pushed himself off the tree and stretched. 'I could join her, too,' through a yawn.

'Don't go to sleep near Djediben. She murdered her second husband, or helped her third husband to do it.'

'Helped Dambena?' he asked, startled.

'Dambena's the fifth, Mabel says.'

'Gosh, what a woman. No wonder Rex is no good.'

'Yes,' she said, her voice far away, 'Rex. What now, I wonder.'

'We'll find out.'

'I must go and see if Mr Heriot has any letters for me.'

'Don't tell him,' Gunn said quickly, 'if he doesn't know.'

She smiled and said: 'I no monkey, brother,' and walked away through the track in the grass, through Heriot's gate, along the path bordered with pink and white vincas. She wore sandals and her legs were tanned; her dark hair was cut short around her neck because of the heat. The watch on her wrist caught the sun and flashed it back to him in time to the swing of her bare arms.

Standing in the shadow of the baobab, feeling the bark with his thumbs, he thought: Why am I always watching them, Helen, Heriot? And where is this point of peace around which I should have my orbit?

At his desk, behind piles of letters, Heriot sat staring at nothing with a blue, veined eye. A cigarette burned away between his stained fingers, his mouth was set in a line that somehow accentuated the unexpected sensitivity of his lips. So far away he seemed that Helen, standing in the doorway shadowed by tall poinciana trees, considered leaving and returning later when he too should have returned to the house of his vacated body.

But his mind came home again, slowly, first noting the filtered sunlight suspending dust above the floor, then her feet, then quickly her face. When he looked into the light his eyes were very old, faded and blue. 'Helen,' he said, slowly. 'I was many miles away.'

'I know, I hated to disturb you.'

'You needn't have. I wanted to be woken.'

'I came,' she said, opposite him at the desk, 'to see if there was any mail for me. Also to ask if you'd slept well.'

He pushed some letters towards her and said: 'Yes, very well. That stuff is good.'

'I hoped it would be. Try it for a week or two, you'll probably feel much better.'

'Why, I'm not sick, am I?'

'No, very well — for your age. But sleep —'

'It is a blessed thing.'

'And no more dreams?'

'Nothing.'

'I'm glad,' she said. 'No need to worry.'

'It's you who worry, Helen.'

'And soon,' she said, 'you'll be free, at last.'

'No,' he said, 'not free, not yet,' looking blindly past her through the door. 'Not as easily as that.'

'How —?'

'Do I know?' he asked, slapping on the desk with his broad palm. 'From this, this effusion from the council. They regret to say they've interviewed the two applicants and found them impossible. One confesses openly he's agnostic, and the other, even worse, isn't one of us at all, he's a lapsed Methodist.'

'Oh, really,' she said, 'that smug little bunch of clerics and do-gooders by proxy —'

But he regretted already having let her see his discontent, and said nothing, only glanced at her with his bitter blue eyes from the depths of silence.

'After so many years,' she said, 'to treat your resignation so lightly —'

'Certainly not lightly. They're treating it very seriously indeed.'

'And aren't you,' she asked boldly, 'aren't you disappointed?'

'Of course. But not,' he said with a faint twist of the lips, 'scandalized.'

She smiled then, catching his eyes, and standing there in front of his table with her letters in her hand, looked suddenly much younger, like a

9

strong-minded schoolgirl. 'You make me sound very bumptious sometimes.'

'I enjoy it. It's unusual.'

A bell rang.

'Breakfast,' he said. 'Young Gunn looks tired.'

'So I told him. He met the boat last night.'

'He's younger than you, isn't he?'

He was stone and iron, she thought, impassive, accustomed through decades to deal with wooings, marriages, disputes. There was nothing which did not concern him, no situation on which he might not be called from his remoteness to arbitrate.

'He's twenty-two,' she said, smiling stiffly. 'I'm twenty-four. And we scarcely know each other.'

'Oh, I wasn't suggesting —'

'I'm sorry then if I —'

Watching the colour deepen under her tanned skin he smiled with genuine amusement, showing the crude, ill-fitting teeth some wandering dentist years ago had made him. 'How suspicious you are, Sister Bond. Do I look like a matchmaker?'

'Anything but that.'

'Too sour, do you think?'

'Too rocklike,' she said, slightly uneasy.

'Like a crumbling cliff?'

'No, not crumbling. A foundation. Or monument. Or something. You're making me feel very bumptious now.'

'Someday I must go,' Heriot said quietly. 'When I do, I like to know — have some faint idea — what will happen after. And who will do it. And all this wretched morning my head's been full of poetry.'

A hen, half-bald, mounted the steps to the doorway, peered in and fled. The flurry of its going merged with the crying crows, the weak and unreal invasion of sound on the earth's essential silence.

'Have, get, before it cloy,
Before it cloud, Christ, lord, and sour with sinning,
Innocent mind and Mayday in girl and boy —'

His voice, husky but not old, proceeded towards the still light which his eyes so intently watched; his hands, moving, burned suddenly in a pool of sun.

No, I won't, she thought, won't be his puppet, won't let him force me into his service. 'Bob Gunn doesn't belong to the mission.'

'He might be persuaded.'

'No, I don't think he would.'

'He seems a good young man. I don't know, it's hard to tell.'

'He wants to go home at the end of the year.'

'Home? What is home?'

10

'I don't know,' she said, strangely tried. 'I really don't know.'

The silence folded itself once more around her words.

'Am I,' he asked after a time, 'keeping you from your breakfast?'

'Perhaps I should be there. Yes.' She turned to the door and stopped, looking down from the step. 'Oh, here's someone waiting. I think I've forgotten his name.'

But though she smiled at him, the dark man outside said nothing. He waited until she had gone, through the patterned shade of poincianas and between the vincas, towards the kitchen. He thought she was pretty and strong and unhappy. Then softly he mounted to the doorway and stood there, with deference, in a patch of sunlight.

The eyes of Heriot, fixed on the floor, took in vaguely the broad black dusty feet. Then mounted to the face.

The eyes of the young man, fixed on Heriot's hand, saw it suddenly tense.

'Stephen,' said Heriot.

'Yes, brother. I come back to my country.'

2

In the eyes of Heriot the young man melted and disappeared and formed again as a bare child, a child with almond eyes and a small hawk nose betraying the distant legacy of an Afghan trader in the blood. But the child was a girl child, so slight, so perfectly formed. There had been a beauty there which hit his heart, now, when it was gone, with a blow of reverberating grief, calling his memory back to that worst bereavement and most bitter defeat which all that morning had been feeding his despair. 'Stephen,' he said again. 'Of course.'

'You know I was coming, brother?'

'Yes, yes, I knew. I'd forgotten. I've been sick, a little bit. You came last night.'

'With Brother Terry, brother.'

'Where are you living?'

'With Ella. She my cousin, brother.'

'Well, you'll have to work and give Ella and Justin some money to feed you. And behave yourself this time,' Heriot said wearily.

'Yes, brother.'

'It's no use saying: "Yes, brother." I've heard that before, too often. You were one I thought I could believe.'

Stephen, in his pool of gold, shifted his feet and searched with his eyes for some place in the room not accusing, not discomfiting. 'Yes, brother.' His voice was low and very calm, beautiful in its accent.

'Why did you do that, Stephen?'

The young man shook his head.

'Why steal when you had a job? You were making more money than your people here have ever seen. Who taught you to be so much of a fool?'

'I don't know, brother.'

'Well, you've finished with gaol now, you won't go back, if you're wise.'

'No.'

'I won't say anything more. But it was a great — a great sorrow to me, to hear what you'd done. Your father was my good friend, my brother. He would have been very much ashamed.'

At this reference to the dead, Stephen moved uneasily. 'Yes, brother.'

'And when he was dead I was your father, and that — that little girl's. I was ashamed. I was ashamed,' Heriot said loudly, staring with his veined eyes. 'And for that little girl, Stephen. Have you forgotten her?'

'No, brother,' Stephen murmured, husky-voiced, tense, wishing to fly finally from this accusing and terrifying old man with his constant talk of the dead. 'Brother, I go now?'

'Yes, go. Have Ella and Justin given you breakfast?'

'Yes, brother.'

'You'll be at the work parade, I'll see you there. No, wait, walk with me to Father Way's house; I haven't eaten yet.' Rising from his chair he appeared larger, broader, wilder-haired than before to Stephen, standing nervously in the doorway. 'You both went everywhere with me once,' Heriot said, coming beside him.

'Yes, brother.'

'You grew up too quickly, Stephen. Do you know how old you are?'

'No, brother.'

'Twenty-two. I remember when you were born. I was your godfather. And the little girl's. And my wife was your godmother. She thought you were handsomer than any baby she'd seen.'

'Yes, brother?'

'But she died soon, she didn't see the little girl.'

They were walking down the road, in the shadow of baobabs, both silent-footed on the soft dust. The village was still, only blue smoke moved now and then upwards from behind mud-brick houses and into the sky, the huge sky.

'Brother,' Stephen said, 'that little girl, she —'

'She's dead. I know. I won't talk about her any more.'

Leaning against a tree farther down the road a man, a black man in a scarlet shirt, waited. 'Does he want you or me?' Heriot asked.

'He want me, brother.'

Uneasy, Heriot thought, always uneasy. What is he afraid of now, why is he always afraid? 'Who is it? Justin?'

'No, brother.'

'Well?'

'That — Rex, brother.'

They had stopped, were standing looking towards the long-legged man down the road, Heriot so still that Stephen grew desperate, would have liked never to have taken the brown tide home to his country where Heriot was. 'Brother —' he said.

Heriot turned on him savagely and seized his arms. 'Who brought him here?'

'Brother Terry —'

'Who told Brother Terry he belonged here? You did. Didn't you?'

'Brother, I —'

'Who did you steal for?'

'I di'n't steal for nobody.'

'Oh yes you did,' Heriot said quietly. 'Rex told you. Didn't he, Stephen? Rex is your *djuari*, isn't he? Your devil-devil, you do what he tells you.'

With Heriot's veined eyes boring into his, Heriot's thumbs boring into his flesh, the dark man weakened, dropped his calm, and became a frightened boy, begging: 'Brother —'

'You ought never to have seen him again, you ought to have hated him for what he did to Esther. Oh, I'm not afraid to say her name, I'll say it again, Esther, Esther, Esther, and hope her spirit comes back to curse you for a bad brother. Rex killed Esther, you know that.'

'No, no, brother —'

'He killed her. In spite of everything I could do. And God knows I tried hard enough to stop it, tried to send him away, tried to talk her into sense. But there wasn't anything I could do, was there?' demanded Heriot, suddenly pleading. 'Not when she was pregnant. I couldn't stop it then. And he took her away, and she died. From neglect and hunger and his beatings. I know that, I know it from a white man. And yet you, Stephen, her own brother, you do what he tells you, you follow him round —'

'He my brother,' Stephen protested shakily.

'The man who killed your sister. And will ruin you yet. I hear more than you think, Stephen. I've heard Rex talking about the wicked white man and the smart black man, and how to talk to the white man and how to get money from him without working. But Rex isn't clever enough for that, and nor are you. You'll end up in a filthy camp, like Rex, like Esther. Stephen,' said Heriot, with grief in his voice, 'don't forget Esther.'

Down the road the tall man came forward from the tree and stood watching them, trying to hear some words of the dispute which was indubitably about himself.

'Brother, I go now,' Stephen murmured.

'Yes, go,' Heriot said remotely. 'I'll talk to Rex.'

He stepped forward down the road to the bright-shirted man. The sun stung his eyes bitterly, but he no longer felt old, only angry and grieved, and very strong. The man's face, looking towards him, was bearded, and both beard and hair had been trimmed with moderate care. As he was tall and had features fairly fine for one of his race, and as there was arrogance in every line of his lean body, Heriot could see with his dazed eyes something of the force in him that had captured the dead Esther. *Ai lewa, walwal*, Heriot whispered; dog, foul man.

Rex said quietly: 'Good day, brother.'

'You've come back,' Heriot said, turning away from the sun and fixing his eyes on the man's.

'Yes, brother.'

'The boat will probably go in again on Sunday night. You'll go with it.'

14

'I bin told I come here, brother.'

'Who told you?'

'Mr Henryson say if you don't tell me I can come after them letters I write, I better go down and ask the white man on the boat when he come next time. And Brother Terry, he say all right.'

Heriot said with contempt: 'I know you get your reputation among your people from pretending to find all the white men at one another's throats. But you're not clever enough to make mischief between the Department of Native Welfare and Brother Terry and me.'

'One time Harry and Maudie come here and you send them away, brother, and that Department Native Welfare, he real wild.'

'Listen,' Heriot said, 'Mr Henryson is my friend. He knows me. He doesn't know you. But I know you. I know you're a troublemaker and a woman-stealer and a lazy, lying blackguard. When you go back I'll write to him and ask him to keep an eye on you, for your people's sake.'

'Might be I make trouble now. All this people here, they my friends, they don't like you send me away.'

'Not many of them, Rex. Why did you come, anyway?'

'This my country, brother.'

'That's not the reason. You're looking for another wife.'

'Might be, brother.'

'Don't call me brother, you're no brother of mine. You killed my little girl, my daughter. I wish to God,' said Heriot, 'Stephen had killed you.'

The tall man, who had been standing partly stooped, hoping to placate Heriot a little with this attempt at humility, straightened and looked at him uneasily.

'I know,' Heriot said softly, 'that sounds strange from me. But I'm very bitter, I'm very bitter, Rex. And I'd see a thousand of you dead if it could bring back Esther. Yes, Esther! Why shouldn't I say her name? I gave it to her.'

In the sun they looked at one another. The light made brown glints in Rex's beard and in his black hair, laid a polish on his skin. Under lids heavy with trachoma, his always wary eyes watched Heriot darkly.

'You're very well dressed,' Heriot said, looking at the scarlet shirt open over his chest, the loose flannel trousers miraculously supported by his hipless body. 'I advise you to go to a station and concentrate on cutting a fine figure of a man on horseback. This place is too poor to keep men who can keep themselves.'

Rex said tensely: 'Thank you, Mr Heriot.'

'Irony doesn't become you,' Heriot murmured, and turned, and began to walk towards the Ways' house. He felt that if for a moment he lost the consciousness of his rocky dignity he would soften and crumble and become an object of pathos and ridicule, calling laughter from the defiant figure behind him; and therefore he kept his shoulders stiff and his stride long and sure.

15

But in the Ways' garden, which was a jungle of poincianas, pawpaws, frangipani, bougainvillaea, and white-flowered creepers, haunted all day by minute finches as bright as any flower, he unveiled to himself his awakened grief for Esther, his disappointment in Stephen, his fear of Rex's influence in the village. He remembered his age and his captivity. 'I could lie down like a tired child,' he said to the birds, 'and weep away the life of care —'

He laughed rustily.

'Any,' asked Djediben, 'dea, *abula*?'

'You've got your tea,' Harris said irritably. 'Go away, now. *Bui!*'

She whimpered at him. 'No dea. More dea, *abula*.' Holding out to him her well-filled tea bag.

'You're a greedy one, Djediben.'

'Ah, *abula*,' she said, grinning hugely with her few tobacco-brown teeth, 'money 'ere, *aru* 'ere.'

From the dirty kerchief round her neck she produced a St Christopher medal, the gift of a Roman Catholic mission far away.

'That's not money.'

She became angry then, and muttered savagely to herself of the avarice of white men, her fingers meanwhile working at a knot in the corner of the kerchief. It gave at last, and two shillings fell on the concrete floor.

'*Aru!*' she shrieked, chasing them, and now happy again. 'I give you, *abula*.'

He took them, hot from her flesh, and weighed out more tea. 'You've got plenty this week,' he said. 'Better give some to the other people.'

'Eh, *nurumal, abula*,' she complained, rubbing her stomach. 'Me 'ungry fella.' But he knew she could be generous.

He looked away from her and wiped his sweating forehead on the back of his hand. 'You go now,' he said. 'You've finished, you've got everything.'

'Djob, *abula*.'

'Soap for how many fella?'

She held up her fingers and counted: 'Midjel. Old man Wunda. Old woman Ganmeri.'

'Yourself, Wunda, Ganmeri,' he muttered, wearily counting out the little blocks of soap. 'That's all now.'

'Grimadada, *abula*. You put 'im in blour.'

He wandered across to the bins and brought back a mixture of cream of tartar and bicarbonate of soda, sprinkled it over the flour in her dirty white bag, and asked hopefully: 'Now we've finished?'

'*Abula*,' she murmured in her throat, drawing out the last syllable blandishingly.

'Well, go away,' he shouted at her. '*Bui!*' And she, without loss of dignity, gathered her bags and went.

In the tin store the heat was stifling. He leaned sweating against his ant-eaten shelves and breathed deeply, longing for a cigarette but not having time, longing for a shower but having to wait till noon. A man of seventy, lean and dry after twenty years in the country, he longed at times for death, but could not die until someone had been found to replace him.

Across the counter Mabel, tall and regal, watched him. She was as old as he and, when tired, sometimes stumbled carrying firewood on her back to the camp. '*Abula,*' she said gently.

When he looked at her he smiled faintly. Her dignity was striking, and on such days, coming to her after the demanding Djediben, he loved her very dearly.

'Good day, Mabel,' he said, taking the bags from her. 'How's your old man?'

'Ah, 'im good, *abula.*'

He gave her flour, tea, sugar, tobacco, working through the list of the indigents' allowance. Potatoes, onion, a tin of milk, some jam, rice, dried peas, porridge, soap. Outside he could hear the other women coming, two dozen of them about to descend on him *en masse.* 'I'd better be quick,' he said. 'I've got something for you. You like *wana,* eh?'

'Yeah,' she said.

So he brought her his half-bottle of honey and put it in one of her bags. 'You got matches?' he asked, knowing how much they were prized, how much labour they saved these old women.

'Madja, *abula,*' she said, holding out her hand.

He gave her half a box from his pocket, and she, gathering up her bags, smiled in her stately and reserved fashion. 'Dang you, *abula,*' she murmured. 'Good day.'

As she went out the crowd gathered at the door, the many old and pathetic, dignified or comic, grateful or parasitical women of his herd, waiting for the weekly rations. Now he would have to run from bin to bin, flat out, in a stream of sweat, for an hour or more in the sweating morning.

He must remember to give them salt to share around, it was the small things that were forgotten on the list. And he would serve the blind woman first.

'Come in, you *ngalis,*' he shouted at them. 'I haven't got all day.'

Outside the meathouse, under the wheeling crows, an old stork-legged man was attacking a cow's head with an axe. He hacked uncertainly at the bone below the horns, one foot on the muzzle, while the beast's eyes gazed as placidly as in life towards the old women gathering up its less edible organs from the grass.

'Here, Wandalo,' Heriot said. 'Give me the axe.'

He held out his hand, and Wandalo, ancient and hesitant, gave it to him. Deadening his senses to the thud of the axe, the feeling of bone shattering under it, Heriot opened the head.

'Now you've got him,' he said, standing back and leaning on the axe.

Wandalo pulled back the top of the head. He squatted with the brains in his cupped hands, dripping blood. The old women in the grass shouted to one another that Abula Arriet had clubbed the beast's head and got the meat.

'You 'id 'im dat bulaman longa *bandi*,' Djediben remarked conversationally.

'Yes,' Heriot said. 'Strong fella me.'

From the hospital rose, suddenly, the sound of singing, the song wild and high, shouted from a strong throat. The old women sat up and listened, screaming excitedly.

'Old man Galumbu,' said Djediben around her grinning teeth. '"Im djingem now.'

'What's he singing?'

'Ah,' she said, 'Derby djong.'

'About the time he was in the leprosarium?'

'Yeah,' she said, 'Derby djong. All time 'im djingem now.'

'Till he gets tired, eh?'

'Yeah,' she shrieked, '"im tired fella by-'n'-by.'

Slowly the crows circled. In the heat the stench of guts struck Heriot a blow in the stomach. 'I'm tired fella myself,' he said 'I'll go and talk to him. Talk to that old man. And sit down.'

'Ah *abula*,' Djediben crooned automatically.

The singing rising and falling tragically in the air, Heriot walked along a narrow path in the grass. Ahead of him a black snake, shining like brand-new pebbled leather, slid across the strip of dirt and disappeared. With each step he took, beads of sweat rolled down the crags of his face and into the damp handkerchief knotted at his throat. 'Tired fella, all right,' he told himself, standing at the gate of the hospital and watching the old man roar his songs from the bed on the veranda. 'Weary, weary fella.'

The old man stopped singing and looked towards him. He had the face of a pleasant child, happy and rather helpless, with his white hair cut by Helen in a fringe, his wide-set eyes staring innocently from below tangled brows. The innocence of the eyes was their emptiness, for he was three-quarters blind, whether from trachoma or from leprosy Heriot no longer remembered.

'*Bungundja?*' demanded the ancient child. '*Gui!*' He was mistrustful of the still figure at the gate.

Slowly Heriot advanced to the veranda, watching the milky eyes for recognition. '*Ngaia*,' he said. 'I. Abula Arriet. How are you, old man?'

Galumbu laughed, gently, a child's laugh. 'Good, bodj, yeah. Good now.'

'You always call me "Boss". You worked on a station once, eh?'

'Yeah, wargam dcidjin, bodj.'

18

'Long time ago?'

'Ah, long dime,' the old man mumbled, his face touched with sadness. 'Binidj now.'

'You're not finished yet. You're good fella, strong.'

The old man lay back with his cheek to the pillow and stared into the light. 'No good. No good now.'

'You're not finished. You'll live a long time with Sister Bond to look after you. Why, I,' said Heriot, with an attempt at humour, 'I'll go to the islands before you, old man.'

Galumbu was silent.

'*Mudumudu,*' Heriot translated. '*Mudumudu-gu ngarambun wanggi ngaia.*'

With a sudden twist of his thin body Galumbu hid his face in the pillow and lay still.

Oh, that I am such a fool, cried Heriot inwardly, such a fool. To mention death, the islands of the dead, here, to him. Oh God, let him not die now, let me not have killed him.

'I was joking,' he protested, '*jagun ngaram, maoba.* Joking,' he said, his voice trailing away.

But there was no persuading the white head to turn and look again at the man who spoke of death, and of his own death, with such lightness, defying the spirits to descend on him and send him on his last long journey to the far islands. Galumbu was turned to stone.

Guilty, uncertain, Heriot moved quietly away and went to the dispensary, where Helen, unexpectedly, sat rolling bandages in her brown hands. He watched her for a moment, the hands and the dark head bent over them, and said: 'Helen.'

She looked up inquiringly. 'Hullo.'

'The old man's not well.'

She stood up, absently disposing of the bandages. 'I noticed he'd stopped singing. But he seemed happy a few minutes ago.'

'I upset him, I'm afraid. I talked about dying. Perhaps you could do something with him.'

Because he seemed uneasy, even a little ashamed of the effect his joke had had on Galumbu, she was sorry for him, and glad to be, since all that morning his lofty cross-examination on the subject of Gunn had rankled, and sitting there with her bandages and with nothing to occupy her mind but Heriot she had felt herself growing steadily more resentful. So she said: 'I'll go and speak to him.'

He sat down on the chair when she had gone out, picked up a bandage and idly began to roll it, feeling useless and old. Most of the men had gone with the tractor to get more stone for the new building; Dixon and Way were superintending the roofing of the finished part, Gunn was in his schoolhouse, Harris in his store. But for Heriot there was nothing to do but wander round his village and wait for the next schedule on the wireless. But tomorrow, he thought, he would go with the tractor, he would gather stones himself, he was strong, his heart was good, there was nothing wrong with him but this tiredness of the mind, this throbbing resentment and desolation. And tonight he would write a letter demanding more staff, two youngish men. He would say it was absurd, the only young man he had was Dixon, and if they were all young the place would still be under-staffed. He would say that he had had enough of being the forgotten man in the forgotten country, he wanted attention and co-operation. He would offer even to withdraw his resignation if only he could have two new men. Then perhaps he would have a chance of getting something done about the cattle. As it was, too much of his time was taken up with paper work, he had no opportunity to think of it. Oh, he'd explain to them, he'd tell this distant council a thing or two.

Helen came back and stood at the doorway, looking brown and cool. 'Galumbu's forgiven and forgotten,' she said. 'A bit of faith curing on my part. He's shaken off his miseries.'

'I'll go back for a moment, then. Thank you, Helen.'

'Thank you for the bandage,' she said lightly, taking it from him.

'Have you — I wonder if you could lend me a cigarette? I've left my tobacco, I've nothing to give the old man.'

She pulled a packet from the pocket in her skirt and gave it to him.

Outside on the veranda Galumbu was sitting up in his bed again, and watched without expression as Heriot dimly approached, and sat down on his bed, and lit a cigarette. His cloudy eyes watched the smoke drift from the white man's lips into the sunlight.

'You want a smoke?' Heriot asked tentatively.

'Djmog? Yeah.'

Heriot lit a cigarette and pushed it between the open lips, and the old man, staring at nothing, his crooked hands on his chest, slowly puffed. Meanwhile Heriot watched the old women, across the grass at the meathouse, and thought of misery and hopelessness, of the wretched tribe of indigents. But it is their choice, their own choice....

He became conscious of the smell of burning and turned back to look at Galumbu. The old man had not moved, still lay gazing into nothing-ness; but the cigarette had fallen from his mouth on to his hand, and the smell was the smell of burning flesh.

'Old man,' said Heriot, very gently, 'I'll give you your smoke.'

He took the cigarette from the crooked hand, long paralysed by leprosy, and held it to Galumbu's lips. The old man took half the cigarette in his mouth and puffed. It grew sodden, and his spittle ran down Heriot's fingers.

'All right, old man,' Heriot said when the dry half of the cigarette was burned. 'Finished now.'

Galumbu, resigning it, requested, 'Bumper, bodj,' and Heriot, after stubbing it, placed the butt in the open mouth. The old man chewed it contentedly.

To himself Heriot murmured: 'You've been a fine man in your day, upright and intelligent, a fine man. And I don't know that we can produce another Galumbu. That's my fear.' Galumbu ruminated, oblivious.

'But to see you now, you and the others — blind or crippled or paralysed with leprosy — thin, covered with sores — flies and trachoma in your eyes. Living with dogs in filthy humpies and refusing anything better — reinfecting yourselves with all the diseases we cure you of... Wretched to be old in your country, old man.'

The old, dark face showed no light of interest.

'I must go,' said Heriot, rising. 'Good day, old man.' He stubbed out his cigarette and put the butt in the old man's mouth. 'Good day, old brother.'

****

— Keep me as the apple of thine eye.
— Hide me under the shadow of thy wing.

The church shuffled, murmured, giggled, muttered deep responses, burst suddenly into singing. The little girls sang high, loud and raucous. The men sang deeply, harmonizing among themselves.

The Lord Almighty —

The boys grinned over their shoulders at their girls, their fathers.

— grant us a quiet night, and a perfect end.

****

Gunn was sitting reading in his house when a knock came on the door. He shouted: 'Come in,' and a guitar entered, followed by Stephen.

'Ah, you,' Gunn said. 'Whose guitar?'

'Rex, brother.'

Gunn looked away, letting it be clearly seen that he had nothing to say on the subject of Rex. 'So you still play,' he said presently.

'Yes, brother.'

'Learn any new ones — where you were?'

'I know plenty now, brother. I sing you that *Old Wagon*, eh? Real nice one that.'

Pushing his book away, a trace of resignation in his voice: 'Yes,' said Gunn, 'sing that one.'

'I sit on you bed, brother?'

'Go ahead.'

But once seated on the bed with the guitar across his thigh, Stephen made no movement to play, only fixed his deep and shining eyes on Gunn's and searched for something there with an embarrassing intensity. Gunn looked away again. After a moment he asked casually: 'Glad to be back?'

'Yes, brother.'

Another silence struck.

'Brother —'

'Yes?'

'I don't do that again.'

'Do what?'

'Stealing, brother.'

'You'd be a fool,' Gunn said shortly. He was helpless to deal with this sly child who in the next few days would be doing the rounds of the whites who had once believed in and helped him. He could hear the same words addressed ingratiatingly to each in turn, to Helen, to Harry, to himself, and the same glance, though for Helen it would be more melting. 'I suppose by now you've forgotten all Sister Bond and I taught you?'

'No, brother.'

'Good.'

'Brother —'

'Well?'

'You ask Brother Heriot not to send me away?'

'He won't send you away,' Gunn said. 'How about singing your song?'

The dark head went down then, the dark fingers worked nimbly at the neck of the guitar. After a bar or two Stephen began to sing, mainly to himself, his hill-billy song of some white man's boyhood. He sang well, his voice clear and firm, and he was also an actor able to fill his singing with surprising nostalgia. Watching him now, Gunn remembered seeing him in camp corroborees, dancing lithely into the firelight and out again, always in the most prominent position, always the supplest and most histrionic of the group. He could be a ballet dancer, Gunn thought. All that lovely limelight . . .

At the end of the song Terry Dixon came and leaned, long, skinny, and red, in the doorway. 'Didn't think it could've been you, Bob,' he said. 'Knew you never went much on that stuff.'

His eyes wandered to the bed and took in Stephen, uneasily watching him.

'You scared of me, Steve?'

'No, brother.'

'Think I'd go crook at you?'

'No, brother.'

'Don't worry, Rex is the man that did me wrong. All forgotten, anyway.'

'Is it?' Gunn asked.

'My part of it. Free pardon from the old tiger because of inexperience.'

'Quiet,' said Gunn. 'Not in front of the child.'

Dixon grinned. 'I've had him. Thinks he knows the lot. Tell the child to go and stand outside his house and sing *All The Cowhands Want to Marry Heriot* with a big cheerio from a cowhand without any cows.'

'But with pretty heavy hands,' Gunn murmured.

The electric light breathed with the panting engine across the road. Stephen, who had been watching it uncomfortably, stood up with his guitar and said: 'I go now, brother.'

'Stay and sing to Brother Terry, if you like.'

'I better go,' Stephen said, waiting for Dixon to move from the doorway. 'I better look after them little kids for Ella. He my cousins, them little kids.' He was very earnest now, wanting to show Dixon the goodness of his heart, to impress him and receive his forgiveness for having recommended Rex as a passenger on the boat.

'Let the man pass, Terry,' said Gunn.

When Stephen had gone Dixon wandered over to the bed and stretched out, yawning. ''Struth, tired fella. Thought Heriot was going to go lousy at me, but he didn't. Just sat me on his knee and told me to remember it next time.'

'He's not a bad old bloke, if you know him.'

'Not the man I'd pick for my best mate. When's he going?'

'Don't know. Not for a while.'

'Too bad. I tell you what, Bob, they need a younger bloke on this place, someone who knows how to make a spot of money out of it. Cattle's the shot, that's what I keep telling the old man. They worked it before, about twenty years ago. But all he'll say is he's been thinking about it for some time, in a nasty sort of a voice, so I shut up and keep my ideas to myself, the way he wants it.'

Propped on his elbow, staring at the floor, 'I don't know anything about it,' said Gunn. 'But I still don't dislike him as much as you and Father do. Nor does Helen. I don't know about Harry, no one ever knows what Harry thinks.'

'You're going at the end of the year, are you?'

'I think so.'

'Why's that?'

'Just that I never felt I belonged here, on a mission. I'm agnostic, to start with.'

'So was I, when I was your age,' Dixon said.

Gunn smiled faintly behind his supporting hand. 'How old are you, Terry?'

'What would you reckon?'

'Might be twenty-five, might be thirty-five.'

'Thirty-two.'

'What turned you Christian?'

Dixon rolled over on his side and said after a moment: 'That's a rare stinking hair-oil you've got on your pillow.'

'Sorry. Shouldn't ask personal questions.'

'I don't mind telling you,' Dixon said. 'You've seen my sort of bloke around, you know what we're like. Never had much time at school, wander about doing whatever's got a bit of money in it, droving or station work, whatever's going.'

'I know what you mean,' Gunn said.

'Yeah, you would. You can get sick of that by the time you're my age.'

'And that's why you came here?'

'Well, it was like this. One time I was riding up a gully and my horse fell down, broke my leg.'

'Stiff.'

'I was there by myself, just lying there, all night. Getting a bit worried too. So I said: "If I get out of this, I'll never say Jesus Christ again unless I mean it." You know the way you think sometimes. Then I said: "God, if you help me now I'll go to church if I can find one to go to." You know —?'

'Yeah, I know.'

'Well, after a bit I got to sleep and had this dream. I dreamt I went back home again to my mum's place, where we were when we were kids. It was all dark, not a candle in the la-la, as they say. But I went in anyway, and my mum, she's dead, she was standing there in the dark. She said: "Why didn't you bring the kids, Terry?" I said: "Mum, you know I haven't got any kids." She said: "Well, where's the wife, son?" I said: "Mum, I never been married." She said: "Well, what are you doing, what sort of a life are you leading?" I said: "I'm not doing anything, Mum, I haven't got a life." Then I woke up, feeling cold, and the leg yelling at me, and a dingo howling up somewhere, you know how they echo in those gullies. I said: "God, if I get out of this I'll go and do something. I'll work in a leprosarium, if you'll help me." '

Look at me, thought Gunn, listening to this and not feeling smart and cynical. I'm growing up.

'Well, they found me next day and I finished up at Darwin, in hospital. There was two kids from this place there, nice kids; they kept talking about "Mission" all the time.'

'Homesick,' Gunn said.

'Yeah. Well, I kept thinking about it after they went home, and when I got out I came over here and asked the old man if he could use me. Kept me waiting a long time, but in the end he told me to come. So I did. That's the story of it.'

He rolled on to his back and stared at the light bulb. 'I never been sorry. Well, I haven't been here long, have I?'

'I don't think you will be. Won't be sorry, I mean.'

'I like the kids. Some of the blokes are a bit hard to get on with.'

He scratched his head and yawned. A new silence was broken by a knock at the door and a voice calling: 'I come in, *wunong?*'

24

Gunn raised his head. 'Come in, Justin.'

Entering suddenly into the light, feeble as it was, Justin blinked and looked down. He was of medium height, broad-shouldered, greying, a man of forty with the quiet dignity belonging to that age among his race. There might be something a little comic about the thin legs running from his loose shorts into his enormous sandshoes, Gunn thought, but nothing to laugh at in his face. From below the broad overhang of his forehead his eyes looked out with a dark shine, observing in silence, making no comment. Homely, thought Gunn, looking at the firm, thick mouth, the broad nose; homely wisdom, and strength, and pride. He said: 'Good evening, Justin.'

'Good evening,' Justin said, in his deep, quiet voice in which there was not humility but a great carefulness, as if he were afraid that by speaking abruptly he would wound the feelings of the young white man. 'Good evening, brother,' to Dixon.

'How's the world, Justin?'

Gunn pushed a chair towards him, and he sat down, stiffly, being strange to chairs, with his hands firmly on his bare knees.

'I thought you might wander in,' Gunn said, '*wunong.*'

It was their custom to address one another as brother-in-law, since Justin had given Gunn a skin name, a classification in the tribe, which put them in this relationship. And Justin smiled suddenly with his white teeth. 'I didn't talk to you for a long time now, *wunong,*' he said.

'I was going to ask you something. What was it? Ah, I know, about murders. What happens when a man murders someone?'

Justin shifted uneasily. 'How do you mean?'

'Where does he go? Does he run away?'

'He goes to other country,' Justin said, 'that way,' pointing north. 'Lost man's country. He stay in that country.'

'And don't they chase him?'

'Might be *babin* go after him. You know, *babin*, all-round man, real clever man, he could kill him. Or might be they just leave him there, in lost man's country.'

'You're a cheerful joker, Bob,' Dixon complained from the bed. 'What do you want to ask him about that for?'

'Just interested. He doesn't mind. Do you, *wunong?*'

'No,' Justin said obligingly.

'What have you been doing tonight?'

'I been talking with Brother Heriot. He real sad tonight. He been talking with old man Galumbu about this islands, and that old man nearly crying, *wunong*. This old men, they don't like you talking about that.'

Dixon asked curiously: 'What islands?'

'Oh, islands in the sea. Where spirit goes. Spirit of dead man, you know, *bungama.*'

'Where are they, the islands?'

Justin pointed, reluctantly. 'That way, brother. They don't like you talking about it.'

'So a lost man,' Gunn said, 'might go through lost man's country and finish up at the islands.'

'Might be,' Justin said. 'If he dead.'

A small silence came down, and through it Gunn pushed back with another question. 'Ever seen a ghost, *wunong?*'

'I heard 'em,' Justin said uncomfortably.

'Where?'

'Onmalmeri. Where all the people was murdered.'

'When was that?' Dixon asked.

'Nineteen-nineteen,' said Justin promptly.

'When you were just born?' Gunn probed.

'No, I was young boy then. Just before they cut me, you know, and start me being a man.'

'Must have been about nineteen-twenty-seven or twenty-eight.'

'Might be,' Justin allowed.

'Are you going to tell us the story?'

Justin leaned forward, hands gripping his knees. 'Yes, I tell you,' he said. His voice became even quieter, he was a careful story-teller and took pride not only in his narratives but also in their delivery. He fixed his bright, dark eyes on Gunn and Dixon in turn.

'There was two stockmen,' he said, 'in fact, three white stockmen, at Jauada homestead. There was Mr George and two other stockmen. Mr George, he was boundary rider, he went out every morning to see if the cattle was running okay, went out early in the morning inspecting the cattle.

'When he done all the boundary he was heading toward home then. Then he came upon a billabong, saw two old native girls in the water. He galloped up to them and said to them: "What you doing here?"

'The two old native girls, they just look at him, they was in the water getting *gadja,* you know, lily-roots. He ask them: "What you doing here on the cattle boundary?"

'He ask the native girls if they got a husband, he ask them in pidgin, like: "Which way you husband?"

'They pointed, telling him, like: "Under the tree, sleeping." They couldn't understand the English.

'He took the two old ladies where the husband was sleeping, and the white stockman ask him: "What you doing in the cattle run?"

'The old man just look at him, and talk in his language that he come getting *gadja.*

'Then Mr George, he told him that he shouldn't be round here, so he got off his horse and flogged him with a stockwhip. I think he gave him twenty cuts or thirty, he beat him for a long time. He broke his spears up,

26

he broke the bottle spear, and the shovel spear, he broke the bamboo, broke it half-way up the stick.

'And the old bloke looked at him, he was bleeding with the flogging he had, across his eyes, you know. And he turned around and got the shovel spear, he looked at him, and he threw it at him, you know how you throw a javelin, and Mr George got the spear in his lung.

'He galloped as far as from here to the schoolhouse with the spear stuck in his lung, and he dropped dead. It cut his lung open.

'The old bloke went over, looked in his pocket, got some tobacco and matches, got some bushes and covered the body. Then he left him in there and went away with his two old ladies.'

'Later on these stockmen missed Mr George for supper that night. They camped all that night worrying what had happened to him, and they got up early in the morning, and they found a horse with a saddle not far from the station. They walked over and examined the saddle, found blood here and there all over the saddle, drops of blood on the saddle. Then they mounted on their horse and went out searching for the body.

'They went all around the boundary searching for the stockman. Later on they came upon the billabong. When they looked across some of the distance they saw a mob of crows around the body, picking at the body. And they galloped over to have a look under the leaves.

'Couldn't even believe if it was a blackfellow's body or a white man's, couldn't tell the difference. Only one thing that put the pot away, one leaf. There was a leaf sticking on the body, with blood, you know. All the rest of the body was black, but when they pulled the leaf away, they could tell it was a white man then.

'Straightaway that night they went in with the motor-launch, made a report to the police. Then they got two good policemen, troopers from Albert Creek. Then the troopers got together, finding out who done the murder. Couldn't get the evidence who done it, so they made their way towards Dampier River.

'Then they brought the troopers to where the body was, and they buried the body and went to the station in the town. So they couldn't get the right culprit, the one who done the murder.

'So they started shooting natives from Jauada all the way up to Dampier River. So many hundred at Jauada, women, men, and children. And all along the Gulgudmeri River. At Onmalmeri there was people camping near the river. They shot the old people in the camp and threw them in the water. They got the young people on a chain, they got the men separate, shot the men only. While they was on the chain the policemen told the police boys to make a big bonfire. They threw the bodies in the flame of fire so no one would see what remained of the bodies. They were burned to bits. They took the women on a chain to a separate grave, then the police boys made a big bonfire before the shooting was. When they saw the big flame of fire getting up, then they started shooting the women.

'When they were all shot they threw them in the flame of fire to be burned to bits.

'When they finished at Gulgudmeri River they went all around Dala. They got a mob of prisoners there, Richard was there, he was a little boy then. They got up and brought them to Djimbula — you know, not far from the aerodrome strip there, under the bottle tree. They camped there, ready to send them next morning.

'Then one morning a boy went out from here — it was Michael, you know, he was horse-tailer — and he saw these troopers' camp. They sang out to him. He galloped across, and they told him: "We got more prisoners here. Keep it secret," they told him, "don't let Father Walton know troopers camping here."

' "All right," he told them.

'So he got on his horse, came back into the mission and then reported to Father Walton. Told Walton there was troopers camping down there with a mob of prisoners, native prisoners.

'He ask Michael: "What they going to do to them?" and Michael told Father Walton they were going to get up and shoot them at Gulgudmeri River.

'So Father Walton, and John Gordon, the aboriginal deacon, and Brother Heriot galloped down to the troopers' camp.

'Then Father Walton ask them: "What you going to do with those prisoners?" He knew they were going to shoot them, he told them that they were not going to do that. He told the troopers to set them free, take the right man that murdered the stockman: he was Djodjin, he was in with that mob of prisoners.

'So they brought the native prisoners into the mission compound and freed them, gave them work, and the troopers took the right murderer into the town.

'Then, a good while after, Father Walton dreamed a dream. In his dream he saw the figure of a native getting shot. He was a real holy man, God must have told him to go Onmalmeri way.

'He went up there, told the stockboys that he had a dream that natives got shot. "Up here somewhere," he told them. "I don't know where, but here."

'He had Mr Mason, a detective bloke, he came from Perth, and Thomas, he was police boy. Then they saw the old tracks where the troopers had their camp where they burned the bodies at Onmalmeri. Then they camped at the old camp where the troopers were camping.

'The boy, Thomas Mason, that was what they called him, he said: "There's a big river over here, somewhere on you right," he told them.

'They went over, and: "There's the spot, right there," he told them, "in the rock, right there."

28

'They couldn't find any remain of the body, it was burned to bits. It was very hard for Father Walton to believe. Then he stooped down and scratched the grave to see if any body bone remained. So he couldn't find any bones — he picked up a teeth, one teeth put the pot away.

'He put it in his pocket, held a burial service, and they left the grave. Then they went to Gulgudmeri River, to the main pool, where they dived into the pool and got some bones. Got the bones, put them in a bag.

'They ask the boy, Thomas Mason, if any more graves. He told them: "You see that bough over there, hanging? That's where the women's grave."

'And so Father Walton picked up more teeth, had the burial service, came back to Onmalmeri Station, camped there, and brought what remained of the bones back to the mission.

'Next day they held the burial service up on the hill there, where the cross is. The bones are in a big box, like this. Then after that they made a report to the headquarters in Perth, and the headquarters told them to come down. Father Walton went to Perth with a couple of boys (Albert, you know Albert, he went to Perth with them). The troopers what were shooting the natives, they was in there in the big court. They paid a heavy penalty then, they done their time or something. And Father Walton came back when the case was over to the mission again.'

Across the road the lighting plant gave a sudden roar, and faded. The light bulb flickered and dimmed, very slowly.

'Nowadays,' Justin murmured, 'now, at Onmalmeri, you can hear ghosts crying in the night, chains, babies crying, troopers' horse, chains jingling.' His eyes glowed in the shadows. 'I didn't believe it, but I went there, mustering cattle for droving to the meatworks, I heard it, too. We was camping at Onmalmeri Station couple of weeks. We were there sleeping, still. It was all silence. You could hear woman rocking her baby to sleep, "*Wawai! Wawai! Wawai!*" like this, rocking the baby to sleep. . . .'*

---

*This narrative was taken down verbatim from an account by Daniel Evans of a notorious massacre. Here the names of people concerned and most place names have been altered.

3

Dogs barked, crows cried. '*Bau!*' shouted Djediben, stock-still in the path. '*Gadea brambun.*'

Behind her Helen, carrying liniments and ointments, awaited the evacuation of dogs into the bush for the greater safety of the white woman, the *gadea*. In the morning sun the hills, the trees, the grass glowed with blinding colours. She was aware, in the heat, of the heavy, stagnant odours of the grass and of Djediben.

Shouts came from the camp, and they moved, she and Djediben, through the grass and through the encircling trees into an arena where, outside bough humpies or in the shade of leaves, the old people waited for her, the naked and the blind, with their asking eyes. The sun glistened on dark skin warmly polished like old wood, and the eyes, the many eyes, watched her with liking, but aloofly, since she came as an intruder into their refuge from all the *gadea*. They were the old natives never quite won from the bush, never acclimatized to the huts and the food of the village.

She kneeled beside a naked old man on the ground, said: 'Good day, Nalun,' and accepting his shy grunt as a greeting in return ran her gentle hands over the dusty back. 'Is that sore now? That hurt?'

He told her with nods that it did. 'Rubbem,' he said, grinning.

With the liniment she soothed him, hardly more than a gesture, an apology for her helplessness to cure him. 'Is that good?' she asked, and he nodded, staring straight in front of him. 'You're blind,' she said, with tears unaccountably in her voice, 'blind.' But he, without a movement of the head, still stared, grinning slightly to express his thanks. 'Dear Nalun,' she said, standing.

From outside a humpy Ganmeri called to her: '*Lala! Lala!*' and she went, carrying her bottles. 'Rubbem,' demanded Ganmeri, the old, old woman, dragging her flour-bag dress above her head. 'Ah, good,' as the hands stroked liniment on the black back.

'That's a new sore,' Helen said, pointing to the raw patch on the old woman's thigh. 'More rubbem there.'

She put down the liniment bottle and took some ointment to treat the sore. And as she applied it, talking with the old woman, a pale dingo pup crept around, peering at her, and upset the bottle.

'Ah!' screamed the women as the fluid drained into the ground. 'Ah!' they shouted angrily at the dog.

The little dingo from running aimlessly burst suddenly into heart-cracking flight, its tail down. The men roared and the women screeched with laughter. Terrified by the uproar behind it the dog, twisting past trees, dodging humpies, dived at last, swift as a snake, into the sanctuary of the grass.

On her knees in front of the old woman, hearing the laughter wash in waves round her: It was such a small thing, thought Helen; and they of all people should have the least laughter. But I have less. I would, if it came to it, have less.

Over Heriot's head the men perched on the frame of the new building, assured as monkeys, fixing sheets of iron to the skeleton of the roof. Their quick laconic remarks and directions to one another fell around him like leaves from the barren branches on which they clung, and he, so alone in their company, so small in their eyes from their high seats, went to find Way, where, in the shade of the baobabs, he stood supervising the laying of foundations for the other part of the building.

'They're doing well,' Way said, removing his linen hat and wiping his forehead. 'It won't be long now.'

Heriot stared at the bent brown backs. 'I hope it will be finished before I go. It would be — something.'

'You're a grudging chap,' Way complained lightly. 'It would be a great deal to everyone, I should think. Quite a handsome building, for us.'

'That was what I meant. To leave just as a new building's finished — very satisfying.'

'Your monuments are all around you,' said Way courteously.

Heriot received that with a meagre smile. 'I'm afraid to you my monuments must look pretty shabby. But when I think back to my earliest memories of the place, and when I remember what old Walton told me of the beginnings, then it does seem something great was done, at some time, by someone. . . . But not by me.'

'That's nonsense, surely.'

'No. All my reign has been marking time. Depression, then war — very little ever achieved. And now, with the Government giving more money than we've ever had, we're still poor. Nothing seems to grow but problems.'

'Which, particularly?'

'The people,' Heriot said, with a shrug. 'As they lose simplicity they lose direction. So what are we going to do with them? Who's going to teach them trades, give them confidence in themselves? Drive them out of this inertia they fall into now their pride's grown enough to make them want above everything to have some sort of *competence*. I don't know the answers.'

'We're promised a technical school, some day, somewhere within a few hundred miles.'

'I wish it well,' said Heriot. 'And you. Because you're coming to the most heartbreaking phase in the history of this problem.'

'We'll do our best, I hope.'

'I hope,' echoed Heriot, and looked at Way, that capable midde-aged man, reflectively and approved him. 'You've time, I think, to see enormous changes, perhaps the end of physical misery among them, as the old ones die out in the way we old ones do. But in the end you'll have something else to face — misery of the mind. And that will be hardest, Way. It's come already. You know Stephen.'

'It could be the whole world you're talking about. The same's true everywhere — the same problems. The worst thing, I suppose, so far, is this long cold war in the towns between black and white.'

Watching the long motions of a man on the roof silhouetted brownly against a cloud: 'Oh yes,' said Heriot, 'oh yes. This is my microcosm.'

Never before in their uneasy, sometimes angry association had they been so much at peace with one another as at that moment in the shadow of the baobabs, watching the man's slow movements on the roof, listening to the slower ring of hammers echoing from beneath it. In Heriot's eyes Way had suddenly grown, had become a figure of hope and of foresight, fit, if he should propose himself, to take over the torch, the helm, whatever rhetorical term you liked to apply to it, of the small world so long of Heriot's governing. And Way, for his part, discovered without warning such springs of warmth and depths of seriousness in Heriot that he was left silent for a time with the awe of revelation.

'I'm very glad,' he said, when he saw Heriot did not mean to go on, 'very glad to have heard your ideas on this. Because none of us, you know, have ever had much conversation with you about the place.'

But Heriot had withdrawn again, had no more to say than: 'Well, I'm sorry for that.'

From his lethargy, brought on by peace and the heat of the day and the languid movements of the figure on the roof, he was dragged back by the sight of a man sitting on the ground inside the building and apparently asleep. 'Who's that?' he demanded abruptly.

'Where?' asked Way, too casually.

'There, sitting down.'

'That man? Rex, I think.'

'Why isn't Rex working?'

'I thought you were sending him back at the week-end. So he can't be employed —'

'I told someone, you or Dixon, he was to work this week, and his wages were to go to Gregory to pay for his keep.'

'I can swear,' Way said, flushing a little, 'you didn't tell me.'

'Why do you let him hang around like that, in any case? Didn't you give him something to do?'

'I suggested a job for him, but he refused, and I couldn't see any reason for making an issue of it.'

Now they were facing one another, the craggy face and white mane of Heriot against the smoother head and features of the clergyman, both burning suddenly in mutual defiance. 'I'd have thought it was a matter of common sense. You know someone must be feeding him,' said Heriot acidly.

'Don't you think perhaps you're too much down on Rex?' Way quietly suggested. 'It begins to look a bit like victimization.'

For a second Heriot stared widely at him, then swung away and went quickly to the building, shouting: 'Rex!'

Rex got nonchalantly to his feet and turned to face him. 'What that, brother?'

'Father Way told you you were to work. Why aren't you working?'

'I don't get no pay, brother.'

'Your pay will go to Gregory. Do you expect him to keep you for a week?'

Rex said with sweet reasonableness: 'I give Gregory my big cowboy hat, he don't want money. You ask him, brother.'

Baffled then, knowing that Gregory would support this statement under torture, Heriot's anger broke out in a shout unsteady with mortification and defeat. 'Get up there,' he ordered, pointing absurdly to the watching men on the house-frame, 'quickly, before I have you whipped.'

Across the face of Rex as he turned away, and across the faces of the men, a slow grin flickered. Twenty years ago, or even fifteen, this threat from Brother Heriot might have been dangerous; but the old man was weak now and had changed, or perhaps all white men had changed, at all events the whip was gone, and the old man's almost unheard-of weapons of expulsion and wage-stoppage were powerless against Rex. They watched him, their clever black kinsman, climb with leisurely insolence towards them, and struggled with a mounting laugh.

Absurd, impotent, Heriot turned away. Behind him, Rex settled himself comfortably on the skeleton building and fostered with a gesture the slow laughter rising in the men. Way watched, still beneath his tree. The men at work on the foundations straightened their backs and looked.

'Get on with the work,' Heriot snapped at them.

He met Way's glance fiercely with his aroused eyes. 'Well?' he demanded.

But from Way there was no protest, only in his face regret that the veteran chief of a moment ago should have shrunk so catastrophically into a petulant child. 'Hate is ruinous,' he said sadly.

From the water flagged with lily leaves, lilies flowering among them, birds rose in sudden stages with a clatter of wings. Ibis and white cranes climbed slowly, wild ducks sped low over the water with a confused whistle, and wheeled, and returned, and flew off again. Geese trailed their long cry over the plain, a single black jabiru following.

Before they had gone the children were already in the water, floundering among the lilies, crying to one another of the coolness of it and of its richness in ducks and flowers. The small children danced naked in the shallows with shining skins. The others, in brief pants, some girls in their dresses, dolphined among the lily stems.

Gunn, seated on one arm of a baobab grown after centuries to resemble a clump of gigantic bagpipes, watched them with contentment. In the rays of the low sun the petals of lilies shone almost translucent against the shadowed hill, the far bank with its leaning pandanus. In that light the lily pads and the reeds glowed green as malachite, the water glistened, rock burned redly on the hilltop. Smooth as a fish, her wet hair flattened, a brown child turned in the water with her arms full of flowers.

He had brought a book with him, meaning to read there, to show Helen that he was not letting his brain lie fallow, but he could only sit and look at the children and the water and the flowers, in a mind-draining peace.

On the lying-down tree, behind his back, he heard the whisper of bare feet on bark, but did not turn. Then two wet brown arms holding long-stemmed lilies came round his neck. 'Ah, brother,' a soft seven-year-old voice crooned lovingly.

'That's Jenny,' he said, trying to look at her.

She giggled, the water dripping from her hair on to his neck.

'Pretty flowers,' he said.

'You want one, brother? They good. You try,' she insisted, pushing a fleshy stem between his lips. 'Chew him, brother.'

Since the stem was already in his mouth, making it impossible to refuse, he bit off a piece and chewed it. It was tasteless, or perhaps faintly sour.

'That good?' she asked.

'Yes, good,' he said, with the chewed green strings in his mouth and not knowing what to do with them. He spat them out.

'You want more?' she invited generously, trying to force another stem into his mouth.

'No, no more,' he managed to say, 'thank you.'

'Ah, brother,' she murmured, and slid around his shoulder to sit down in front of him on the tree. They looked at one another with mutual amusement, he taken with her thin limbs and white teeth, she with his sunburned face and lank hair.

A boy crouching under the leaning tree tugged at her hanging leg. '*Ali!*' she cried, with exaggerated alarm. 'That Normie, he pull my leg, brother.'

34

'Come out, Normie,' Gunn ordered.

The small boy appeared and leaned grinning against the tree. 'I don't hurt her, brother,' he protested. 'Brother, why you don't go swimming?'

'I'll swim another time.'

'There big snake in that water, brother.'

'What, now?'

'Might be. I don't know, brother. Edward, you know Edward, he were after duck one day in the water and that snake, he bite Edward leg, just here, brother. Edward reckon that old snake after them duck too.'

'Wasn't it poisonous?'

'I don't know, brother. But Edward, he come running out of water pretty quick, and he look at his leg, brother, and there that old snake teeth sticking there in Edward leg. Real big teeth, brother.'

'He must be a tough man.'

'Ah, he real tough. He real cowboy, brother.' Normie laughed, leaning against his tree, to think of the heroic toughness of Edward.

Gunn was looking absently towards the far blue hills. 'I'd like to go there,' he said, 'there, past the hills.'

'That cowboy country there, brother.'

'Everything's cowboy country to you, Normie.'

'All hill and rock there. Plenty kangaroo, brother. Only old people go there, not mission people. He real lonely, all that country.'

'I know,' Gunn said meditatively, turning his eyes back to the pool where three girls were chasing a boy through the rafts of leaves and flowers, they screaming, reaching, he laughing over his shoulder and shining with water-beads. 'No sense in being lonely, is there?'

Outside the store, sitting or standing in the dust in their usual after-work groups, the men and Dixon looked at one another and laughed.

'Brother,' shouted Stephen, bent in the middle with histrionic amusement, 'I go right over your head, brother!'

'Well, I went right over Gregory's head,' Dixon said, 'and landed on mine.'

Gregory laughed deeply from his fat chest. 'I thought I were going to sit on you, brother. But then I thought I pretty heavy for Brother Terry, and I don't do that then.'

'Good on you, Gregory. I'd be thinner now if you had.'

On the way to collect a load of sand the trailer had become uncoupled from the tractor, catapulting its passengers in a long arc to the ground; and part of their amusement was the thought that if the tractor had been travelling more slowly it might now be decorated with several sets of brains. 'Ah, brother,' said Michael, in a deep burst of laughter, 'you looked funny. You flying down like a duck, brother.'

Matthew, the most serious of them, looked up from tracing designs in the dust. 'Mary's husband, he was working in town and trailer tipped over. Killed him. Reckon Mary would get money, but she didn't get much. Not like white man's wife.'

Dixon moved uneasily. 'That was bad luck.'

'Like they say, brother, one law for white man and one law for black man. You reckon,' on an inquiring inflexion, 'eh, brother?'

Dixon hesitated, unhappy at the question, knowing a flat disagreement would alienate them, agreement only foster their resentments. He muttered: 'I don't know, Matthew. That was a long time ago, was it?'

'Yeah, long time.'

'It wouldn't happen now. That bloke who lost his leg got a lot of money. I forget how much, but a white man wouldn't have got any more.'

Michael said: 'Someday we all be citizens, eh, brother?'

'Yeah, some day you will. You got to work for it.' But I can't preach, he thought, no good me trying to talk to them. Nobody tries to talk to them, nobody tells them the whole thing. That's what Heriot ought to be doing, or Bob, not me, I don't know anything.

'I better go for my tucker,' he said, turning away. 'See you in church, some of you.'

They watched him silently, with expressionless faces, while every word he had said and every opinion he had betrayed was sorted and weighed and stored for the future in the tribal archives, their disoriented and searching minds.

In his office, still but for the continual flutter of moths about the light globe, Heriot sat drafting his letter. He would stay, he said with humility, he would stay, since he seemed to have no choice in the matter. But he must have, he needed, he could not go on without more staff. Please, he said, do not ignore this most serious request, or the people and the place will suffer for it; old men cannot hope to deal with all problems, not in this uneasy time.

As he sat there looking over his letter, his face glowing red-brown in the yellow light or eroded with great shadows, a knock very faintly sounded through the door, and he sighed, recognizing the timidity of a black hand and fearing some crisis in the village. He rose, trod heavily to the door, and opened it. A rough wind was punishing the trees, and a swirl of leaves and dust followed the swing of the door into the room. The light fell on dark, waiting faces.

'Gregory, is it? Michael? Richard? Something wrong?'

Gregory hitched up his shorts, a gesture of nervousness. 'Nothing wrong, brother. We want to talk with you, please.'

'I see. Well, come in,' Heriot invited, standing away from the door. 'Sit down.'

They sat, stiffly, on the chairs in front of his table, and he went, also stiffly, to his own. Eyes questioned across the littered desk.

'Well,' he said, with vitreous geniality, 'here you are, my three counsellors, my village politicians. What have you come to talk about?'

Their silence lay in front of him like a black cloud. 'Come on, now, Gregory,' he said. 'What is it?'

Gregory moved tensely in his chair. 'It Rex, brother.'

'Oh,' said Heriot softly, 'Rex.' He played with a pencil, rolling it under his broad-tipped fingers. 'Well, what about Rex?'

'We don't reckon you ought to send him away, brother.'

'And why,' asked Heriot woodenly, 'do you reckon that?'

Richard said suddenly and with released anger: 'You not fair, brother. He not a bad man, Rex. You don't give him no chance. He just want to live here, in his own country, and work for mission, get married might be. What for you want to send him away now?'

'For exactly the reason you came here tonight. He makes trouble. He's been talking to you, hasn't he? He told you to come and see me.'

Michael murmured: 'He real sad, brother, leaving his country.'

'The first time he left it, it was because he wanted to. I told him not to take that girl, his wife, away from here. I got angry with him. But he wouldn't listen, he left, and the girl, too. What does he want here — to find another girl and take her away and kill her?'

'That girl die, brother,' Gregory protested. 'No one kill her.'

'I won't argue about that.'

In the silence that fell again Heriot struggled with his anger and his uncertainty, thinking: But I am not unfair, no, I'm simply the one person who can see through Rex and has learned to distrust him. And look, here; already he has set my people against me.

'You hard man, brother,' Richard said.

Was hard, yes, when there was need for it; but not now, no, they're hard on me now.

Michael said indifferently: 'Some people in the village pretty angry.'

Oh yes, I can see them, the young ones, sitting outside the firelight discussing my sins, growing angry, and laughing, and growing angry again. And Rex playing the oracle, and Stephen playing the guitar. I can see them.

'What does Justin say?' he demanded.

'Justin?' asked Gregory uncertainly. 'He don't say nothing, brother.'

Richard said with faint contempt: 'Justin, he real old man. He don't listen to Rex.'

Good Justin, most conservative, most loyal friend, resisting change. But I am not. I'm not shutting out the future, there is no future in Rex. Rex is only anarchy. Justin knows this, but how could he side with me against all his people? He's waiting for me, he wants me to be strong. Many of them must want it, many women especially would rather see Rex away.

'Rex is leaving on Sunday,' he said.

Michael and Gregory said nothing. But Richard, with angry eyes, burst out: 'Might be all the people hate you now, brother. Might be no one working for you tomorrow.'

Still rolling the pencil under his fingers, Heriot said very quietly: 'I've heard that in other arguments, Richard, but you know nothing comes of it. You haven't a card to play against me. That's the only thing that worries me, I've every opportunity to be unjust. But I don't think I am. I pray to God,' he said, in a curious, empty voice, 'to guide me, and I couldn't go on unless I thought He did. I hope this is the last I'll hear of Rex.'

He looked down at his fingers. After a pause, 'Brother,' Gregory said, tautly and uneasily.

'Well?'

'If Rex go away, we going too, and our wives, and our little kids.'

In silence Heriot stared at them, the three of them, who for several years had met with him there, sat in the same chairs, and discussed problems of the settlement, problems of people, ideals and desires and needs and amusements of black and white, always with trust, courtesy, and keenness, always deeply serious. 'No,' he said.

'We got to go, brother, if you do this.'

'I won't be bluffed,' Heriot said. 'Do you hear that? I won't be blackmailed. I'm not a child or a fool.' From his tiredness and his indecision he was raised, burning with anger. 'I've given more than thirty years to serving you people, almost half my life. Do you think I can be discouraged so easily?'

They said nothing.

'Do you see that photograph, there, on the wall? Who is it?'

Gregory muttered: 'That you wife, brother.'

'Yes, my wife, you remember her. Sister Margaret. She had beautiful hands. You remember her hands, don't you, tying up your sores and bathing your eyes and playing with you when you were children. You haven't forgotten that. And when you were young men, you remember her getting thinner and thinner and not smiling much and going to bed and dying, and your mothers going up and down outside the house, crying and wailing all night and all day, while I sat there beside her, trying not to hear them, trying to believe I couldn't have saved her by taking her away from this country. No, you haven't forgotten that.'

He glared at them with his ancient eyes. 'You see that other photograph, those children. Who are they?'

Out of his rigid silence Michael half-whispered: 'That Stephen.'

'Stephen, and Esther. Esther Margaret, my daughter. Rex's wife. You remember her, too, how graceful she was and how much she laughed always, in that husky voice, and her singing, and that little gold chain she wore round her neck, my wife's chain, and played with when she was talking to you. And her beautiful writing, and the way she'd read stories to your children and teach them to draw. And you remember how she began to meet Rex, at night, hiding behind trees down by the river, until she was past escaping. And how he married her and took her away, and how he killed the child in her, and killed her with it. But you must have forgotten that, or you couldn't be wanting him to stay here.'

Their eyes stayed blankly on him.

'I've given half my life,' he said softly. 'My wife gave all of hers. I've lived in poverty, half-starved at times, been lonely, been overworked, been forgotten by everyone in the world except you. For twenty years the only happiness I've had has been when, for a day or a moment, you and I have come suddenly together, in friendship. You must believe, when I say that, that I wouldn't part with your friendship for anything in the world less than your own good.'

But I have done wrong, he thought, to boast of my sacrifices, bludgeon them for their gratitude. Now surely I've grown old. There was never, never before, such self-pity in me; I am ashamed.

Richard said in a hard, flat voice: 'Brother, we didn't choose you.'

But Gregory and Michael, moving uncomfortably on their chairs, dissociated themselves from him. 'You always been our friend, brother,' Gregory murmured.

Weariness, and a desire to smile, even, irrationally, to laugh at them, overcame Heriot now that his tirade was over. He pushed away the pencil.

'I think you should go,' he said. 'You know what I'm going to do. There's no point in talking about it now.'

He stood up, and they, irresolutely, followed suit. He opened the door and watched them step down to the rectangle of light on the dust, and turn there and murmur automatic good nights from the edge of darkness.

What they were thinking mattered suddenly very little to him. Standing there in his doorway he was concerned with the wind and with the lightning that from time to time cracked the dark-clouded sky. As he watched it his hands grew calm again, he found peace in its purpose, in the remote and unfathomable justice of its occasions.

4

In the morning lightning struck the grass behind the store, causing a small fire. The men beat it out, shouting and laughing to one another against the wind. Dust blew down the road and moved across the plain, looking white and solid in the cloudy light. The air was suddenly cool.

'There's been a cyclone warning,' Heriot said, treading grit on the office floor, 'but we should be out of it if it goes the way they think.'

'We seem to be getting the edge of it,' Way considered, looking at the dust.

'We've never been hit in the time I've been here. Hope our luck's still in. If a bad one came, I'm afraid we'd have to rebuild the whole place.'

Way said: 'Don't say that, brother,' mimicking the superstitious uneasiness of a native. 'Myself, I feel much the same as the people do when it comes to tempting providence.'

Heriot reached out after some straying papers and tucked them away, listening to the uncertain wind, hearing outside dry poinciana pods fall down rattling to the ground. 'You could,' he said, without interest, 'have a service in the church and pray for the cyclone, if it is one, to go somewhere else. Into that country out there, where it can't hurt anyone.'

'I could,' Way agreed. He watched Heriot sit down and begin to roll a cigarette. 'You don't seem very worried.'

Heriot's fingers, against the white paper, were stained darkly with nicotine, the nails black-rimmed. 'Fatalism,' he said. 'And I'm tired.'

'Would you like —?'

'No.'

'Surely today, though, you can rest.'

'It's not rest I want,' Heriot said flatly. 'I don't know what I want.'

'I can cope, you know.'

'This morning I woke up — grieved that I wasn't dead —'

'So there's really no need —'

'Ninety or a hundred years old, and very cynical, very bored —'

'Sorry, I didn't hear.'

Dust blew in. 'I was talking nonsense,' Heriot droned, 'for my own entertainment. Old as Tiresias, but very stupid. When is my spring coming?'

'Classical allusions?'

'I'm a very small fraction of a scholar,' Heriot said, rasping in his dry throat. 'Why do you stay here listening to me? I've got nothing to say. I can sit here all day happily complaining to myself about unhappiness.'

How can I deal with this? Way thought, keeping his face turned with some firmness away from the eyes of Heriot unreasonably glaring at him. At times I can believe what the children say, he's terrible. 'What's the matter with you?' he demanded, with brave sharpness.

The confronting eyes kindled with a kind of amusement. 'I'm a wicked man who wants to be dead. And hates everyone.'

'Or enjoys pretending he does.'

'There's no pretence. I discovered that last night. For years I set myself up as a philanthropist and was really a misanthrope all the time. Ironic.'

'I suppose there's no reason why a constructive misanthropy shouldn't achieve as much as philanthropy. There's a bold modern view for you.'

'What would you say,' Heriot asked softly, the sour laughter still in his eyes, 'if I said I thoroughly disliked you, and your bold modern views?'

'I shouldn't,' Way confessed, 'faint with surprise. It's been obvious for a long time.'

'I don't think it has. Not to me.'

'Perhaps the rest of us were more observant.'

'You,' Heriot accused gently, 'are beginning to be angry.'

'Not I.'

'The polite charity is peeling off in strips.'

Way's pink face had grown red, and the slight bald patch in his hair also, and his fingers were unnecessarily concerned with the papers he was carrying. But 'Nonsense,' he said, in a firm ecclesiastical voice.

'Oh, yes. I'm being very annoying, I don't know why.'

Dust lodged in Way's throat, and he coughed, and said in a choked voice: 'As a matter of fact I know — know about your outburst to the counsellors last night.'

'Do you, indeed?'

'I can't see any need to brood over it, which is obviously what you're doing. It will probably do them good to be reminded of some of the things the white man has done for them.'

'I'm glad to have your opinion,' Heriot said, smoke wreathing his wooden face, his wooden eyes.

'You're not, but perhaps you need it.'

'Does it sometimes occur to you that I'm a lonely old man who needs someone to discuss his problems with him?'

'Yes, it does.'

Heriot ground out his cigarette. 'It's like your smug impudence,' he said viciously. 'I need no one.'

Way, angry-mouthed, tightened his hands around the papers he was holding, clutching to himself his good temper, his charity.

41

'Will you listen,' Heriot demanded, the toneless voice suddenly broken, uneven, rising to cracked notes of spleen and weariness. 'I'm dying. When my friend, Stephen's father, was well and strong and quite young, he told me he knew he was going to die. And he died. And now I know. And after all these years of being forgotten and ignored, I suddenly find that I resent it. I don't want to pass piously to a quiet grave. I've built something nobody wanted, and now the thing I think would give my life its full meaninglessness would be to smash it down and take it with me. Let them regret it when it's not there if they won't appreciate it when it is.'

'But it's not yours to smash,' Way said evenly.

'I'm the only one of the builders left. All the others are dead. They had my ideas, they made my mistakes, they used the whip sometimes, they were Bible-bashers and humourless clods, they were forgotten while they were alive and attacked when they were dead. You don't like the work we did — very well, we'll take it back.'

'You were founders, you were like coral insects. You can't smash what you've started because you yourself belong to your successors —'

But Heriot halted him, holding up his hand. On the palm lay a small ivory crucifix which he had picked up from the table.

'Do you see this?' he asked, in his new straining voice. 'This.' The uneven teeth showed. 'A little Popish thing from the bad old days of Walton.'

His hand came down sharply on the edge of the table, and he brought it back and flung the pieces towards Way; whose eyes, torn at last from tormented, detruncated head, the outstretched arms of the fragment lying in his lap, lifted again and met his across the table with an expression of incredulous shock.

'I believe in nothing,' Heriot said softly. 'I can pull down the world.'

At the sound of wind and at the fall of the branch the girls screamed like birds, clutched one another, trembled. '*Ai!* Mummy Dido!'

But Dido, huge as a round boulder and in no mood to encourage them, looked placidly over her flock of orphans and growled. 'You girls, you think a bit of wind hurt you? Nothing going to hurt you in this dormitory. Real strong, these walls. You stop you shouting and stay on you own beds.'

Nothing could move her. She took the hand of a small child who was crying. 'What all you girls doing, just sitting there?' she demanded. 'You better sing some songs.'

They shivered as a bough scraped down the roof.

'Ruth,' demanded Dido, 'what wrong with you? You start singing, go on now.'

'What you want us singing, Mummy Dido?'

'You know plenty songs,' Dido said impatiently. 'Ah, you girls, you no good! I going to sing myself.' And the rich voice crooned, 'God that madest earth and heaven, darkness and light —'

At the sound of her voice they took courage, and around Ruth's bed rose a murmur of singing, growing to a raucous shout.

From this valley they say you are going,
We will miss your bright eyes and sweet smile —

Under this opposition Dido faded slowly into silence and sat still, looking out towards the anguish of wind in leaves and branches. She was a Buddha, a round rock, vast and warm and immovable in the knowledge of her responsibilities.

In the swirling dust, at midday, and at the height of the wind, Heriot plodded through the village, his clothes flapping, his wild white hair on end like the crest of a crane.

The village was indoors, sheltering behind its mud walls and threatened roofs from the possible violence about to come. The road was deserted, dotted with small fallen boughs.

Being so alone and in such chaos of air he could have shouted out to the wind that he loved it and worshipped it, that overnight he had become its convert, forestalling ruin by embracing ruin. The wind at least, which knew how to tug and tease a weak branch until it slackened and cracked and fell, would understand him, who had been for a quarter of a century the sheltering tree of this small kingdom and was now, by modern ideals and modern discontent, to be brought down.

Broken. Broken. Broken. On the far shore of the world.

In the breaking of the crucifix he had confessed, at last and forever, the failed faith. Now he could admit to himself that what was once the bright fruit of a young tree had shrivelled and dried and sifted away in the late years of loneliness, and was not to be found again on the ant-bed floor of a church. He cried to himself under the thrashing trees to be taken and broken on the wheel of the wind.

All his age and all his frustrations had come suddenly upon him, he was an old, tired man, though he walked straighter than trees in the dust.

He would take this last walk around his domain, wait for the wind to die, then with all the whites assembled in Way's living room, announce his departure. He had already, soon after Way left him, transmitted his telegram of resignation to the far city. This walk in the wind was his farewell; afterwards there would only be waiting and going.

He found that he was coming to the skeleton of the half-erected building, the last work begun under his command, and made towards it automatically, according to his habit, although there were no workers to check on or progress to admire with the village behind its own walls. As he came driving forward, head down, over the road, a man moved in the shelter of a wall.

'Rex,' Heriot said, stopping sharply. 'Why aren't you inside?'

The man stared blankly at the blowing white hair. 'Why not you, brother?'

'Oh,' said Heriot softly, with his sudden shattering grin. 'So you've quarrelled with Gregory.'

'I got plenty friends, brother.'

Above, on the incomplete roof, a sheet of iron grated and rattled in the wind.

Heriot said: 'That's going to come off in a minute.'

'Might be.'

'You'd better go and tell Brother Terry. He'll give you tools to fix it.'

The eyes of Rex still surveyed him expressionlessly. 'I don't work here, brother.'

'But you'll go.'

'No.'

'Rex — I'm not boss of this mission any more. I'm not ordering you.'

The dark neck moved, the eyes fixed on his with an intenser gaze. 'You going, brother?'

'Yes.'

'I can stay, now?'

'No. You can go away and come back in a year, if you behave well.'

'That no good,' Rex said loudly. 'No good!' The eyes grew larger and burned. 'All this people going with me if I go. You know that, brother.'

He pushed himself away from the wall and came into the wind, his scarlet shirt flapping. And Heriot, flooded with strange compassion, put out his hand and seized the dark arm. 'Understand,' he said gently. 'Oh, but you're lost —'

Rex tore back his arm and stepped away, and stood stooped and fluttering in the dust. 'I don't go,' he said, in his deep broken voice. 'I don't go.'

'We'll speak about it again,' Heriot said. 'Later, later, Rex, when it's calm. I should go,' he murmured vaguely, with the curious excitement in him, turning away.

The wind was reaching its peak, filling the air not only with dust but also with leaves and grass, tearing down branches. The loose sheet of iron clattered on the roof, a continual assault on his nerves. He walked with his head down, his hair tormented into white wisps.

Then on the calf of his leg came an enormous impact, a great numbing pain. He swung round, looking down, and found what he had half-known would be there. The first stone.

The first stone. And across huge desolations towered the figure of Rex, appearing and disappearing through a curtain of dust, his teeth showing in an uncertain grin.

Heriot bent down and took the stone in his hand, heavy, lethal. He was the martyr, struck by the first instrument of execution. The air was full of faces and raised hands. Walking towards Rex he was stumbling through murdering crowds, buffeted with screaming, spat on and wounded. And before all was one face, the dark face with its frozen white grin above the bright shirt.

But he would be no martyr, not submit to these flailings as if owning himself wrong, he would strike back, godlike; not he, but the fierce crowd would die.

He sobbed in his throat. The stone flew.

With a violent gust the wind threw up a white curtain, Rex was gone, vanished in a shroud of dust. Around him Heriot believed he saw dark figures struggling towards him in a dry mist.

He went forward through the haze. Dust already lay thinly in the folds of the red shirt and on the thick flow of blood down the forehead. The man had reeled back, wounded by the stone, and fallen among rocks. There was blood also running muddily down from the back of his head.

Without bending, without touching him: 'Dead,' said Heriot, feeling in himself the thickening of blood, the stiffening and relaxing of fingers. 'Rex —'

He turned and abandoned him, half-running through the wind. With the shriek of a mad bird the flapping iron tore itself free from the roof and crashed among the trees.

When he came out of his house he was carrying his rifle and had thrust a box of cartridges into his pocket where it bulged solidly. There was no expression in his grained, carved, wooden image's face, and no uncertainty in his movements. He walked strongly into the weather and went to the yards where the collected horses shivered and trembled with the wind in their manes and their great eyes on the wind.

He dragged out bridle, saddle, and saddle-cloth from the shed and picked a quiet piebald called Albert Creek, the only horse he knew now in these sedentary days. His hands were very firm with the buckles, but Albert Creek was restless, it took time.

As he quietened the horse: 'Brother,' said someone behind him, and he turned and found Justin standing at the rails, his hair waving on end.

'What is it, Justin?' He was impatient and his eyes were strange and unfriendly.

'I seen you going past my place, brother.'

Heriot reached for the bridle and led the horse from the yard, saying nothing.

'*Nandaba grambun?*' Justin asked placatingly. 'Where you going?'

Slowly Heriot swung into the saddle and towered there with the rifle before him, his shirt and his hair fluttering, but himself as still as a ship's

45

figurehead set on a flinching horse nervous at the ears. He said sadly from the sky: '*Mudumudu-gu ngarambun, abula.*'

'Ah, brother,' Justin murmured, not smiling, 'you got those islands on you brain.'

'I want you to tell nobody, Justin. This is a secret. I need to go now, while the wind's still up.'

'How long will you be, brother?'

'A long, long time.'

'But you come back tonight?'

'I won't come back.'

'But, brother,' Justin asked anxiously, 'where you blanket, eh? Where you billy and you tucker?'

'I'd forgotten them.'

'I go and get them? They in you house, eh?'

'Yes, yes, go and get them, if you like.'

'You got plenty tucker in you little kitchen?'

'Plenty of tucker. It's all yours, as much as you like. But go now, hurry.'

'I hurry,' Justin promised, turning and running back into the gale.

When he was out of sight Heriot kicked Albert Creek into a gallop and ran with the wind towards the giant baobabs of the lagoon. Already the fringe of cyclone seemed to be passing, though the white dust still scudded ahead of him in waves, and grass blew, and the lagoon was a grey sea with all its lilies sunk. There he pulled in to a walk and sat loosely in the saddle, and watched the hills, which were no longer blue but grey and spectral, infinitely far.

He had come five miles across the plain, passing the creeks with their spare cadjiput trees and chapped water, and reached at last a place where the water ran through sand among gums and wattles, a shady forest where he was bewildered by watercourses, crossing one after another and never coming to the last, until he imagined he was on an island circled by seven creeks and could never put out again. But the hills were his aim and the cause of his vast calm, and he was not discouraged. So he reined in there and looked quietly around for a passage from the maze, and while waiting heard behind him a crashing among the fallen branches of wattle. He turned and watched, and saw presently Justin climbing his horse up the sandbank of the last creek.

Heriot's face went perfectly still, was so wooden and forbidding that Justin, coming up on his sweating horse, could only stare at him with timid eyes and was afraid to speak. Until finally Heriot, surveying with the same stunned calm the blanket roll, the old flour bag, the billy and the two spears that accompanied the brown man, asked softly: 'Why did you follow me?'

'You angry, brother?'

'I wanted to be alone. Who did you tell when you left?'

'I didn't tell nobody, brother. First I get you tucker and you blanket and go to the yard, and you gone from there. So I go to my place and get my spears and nobody see me, then I come after you. I only seen you other side of the creek, brother. I thinking you were lost.'

'Yes. You've ridden hard.'

'I take one of you blankets for myself, brother. That all right, eh?'

'Go back, Justin. I'm going on alone.'

Justin asked stubbornly: 'Where you going?'

'You know, I told you.'

'You don't really go to those islands.'

'I'm going to a place no one comes home from. You understand an order, Justin. I don't want you here.'

Justin said, with perfect deference: 'I got to come, brother.'

'Go back to Ella and your children. It's your duty, you understand that.'

'Stephen look after Ella and the little kids, brother.'

'I'm going nowhere,' Heriot said. 'Nowhere,' a desperate anger in his frozen eyes.

'You don't know that country.'

'Nor do you.'

'I been there once, with my old lady, all over up to coast.'

With the rifle weighing like rock across his thighs: 'Listen,' said Heriot in a choking voice, 'I'll get to the hills tonight and I'm going no farther. There's nothing you can do, I don't want you or need you. Or your food or blankets. I need nothing at all.'

The fading wind tossing the wattles over them, they watched one another with such curious intensity that they might have been the two last people left on earth, each hastening to impress on his memory, before it should be too late, the face of the other. Still in his anaesthetized peace of spirit: 'You've brought food,' Heriot said.

'Yes, brother. Tin food here.'

Restlessly the two horses craned their necks towards one another. 'Good,' said Heriot softly.

'Brother —'

They stared hungrily at one another. 'Yes?'

'If you go along with me, I go with you, always.'

Behind the uneasy trees rose the hills, and beyond them again the country of the lost, huge wilderness between this last haunt of civilization and the unpeopled sea.

'Welcome, my Good Deeds,' whispered Heriot. 'Now I hear thy voice, I weep for very sweetness of love.'

Late in the afternoon, under a torn sky, the village woke suddenly into wild mourning. The wailing of women broke out on the wind, mixed with the frightened cries of children. The whites came to their doors and looked out. Gunn and Dixon, emerging from their houses, met in the windy road with a simultaneously shouted question.

They saw by the hospital a little bunch of keening women, their heads bent and covered, and from the gate Helen appeared and came running up the road, her skirt flapping and her smooth hair ruffled by the wind.

As she came up: 'What's wrong?' they demanded, and she stopped, panting a little, and stiff with apprehension around the lips.

'They say Rex is killed,' she said, breathless.

That shocked them, they looked at one another. 'How? Where?' they wanted to know.

'I can't stop. Come with me. They may be wrong, they were about Dicky, remember?' She broke away again, and they ran with her. 'It's at the new building.'

'How'd it happen?' Dixon asked.

'They say a sheet of iron — blew down and — hit him. Oh — terrible if I were late . . . .'

'He shouldn't have been out,' Gunn said.

'No,' she said. 'No.' In front of them was the building, and under a tree a group of squatting men with their heads bowed. They had not known how to take this death, whether to mourn as white men or as black. Though two older men had wounded themselves on the forehead with stones and were quietly moaning, the blood running down, the others were still and silent.

'Over there,' Dixon said. He hung back from her as she approached the body and knelt beside it. Dust lay over the clothes and had crusted thickly on the bloody forehead.

She unbuttoned the scarlet shirt and put her hand to the brown breast. As she held it there she was not looking at the man, Gunn saw, but at something far away or perhaps invisible, and with such passion that he was startled and found her unfamiliar. It was as though she were willing life to push down and pierce through her fingers into the heart beneath them, or as if by concentration she could absorb death into herself and there overcome it. He heard Dixon breathing lightly beside him, and glancing up saw his eyes were fixed on her with puzzled awe.

She said in a toneless voice and without moving: 'He's alive.'

Dixon moved back and cleared his throat. After a pause: 'Thank God for that,' he said sincerely.

She had lifted, very tenderly, the head. 'He'll have to be moved gently. It's dangerous. Would you get some men and go for the stretcher, Terry?'

'Like a shot,' he promised. He went quickly away towards the mourners, shouting: 'He's okay, boys. He's alive. We just want the stretcher.'

They got to their feet and looked at him. There was a silence. Then they began to make comments to one another, then jokes. In a minute bursts of laughter were drifting over from the trees.

Gunn said quietly: 'After a decent interval they'll begin to celebrate.'

'Yes.'

'There's the sheet of iron, over there, by the trees. It must have dropped pretty sharply and been blown along the ground.'

She was watching the quiet dark face. 'I suppose so.'

'You looked — different, just then. We both noticed it. Like a doctor. Or a mother.'

She turned to him for an instant her rapt face, and said in the same remote voice: 'Please, Bob, don't say anything. He's so nearly dead. And this is, really, my first child.'

Before dark Justin and Heriot entered the hills, passing a wide pool at the mouth of a gorge and directing the horses along the flat shelves of rock above it. Beyond the pool, glimmering greyly among spidery pandanus, the stream broke over rapids, the cliffs above grew steadily huger, until there was only a narrow echoing chasm with a strip of grey sky over it and deep shadow filled with the rush of water all around. Great boulders, cast down from the crumbling cliffs, lay across the rock platforms, and the horses slithered and snorted, sliding past chunks of stone twice as high as themselves. In the stillness that overlaid and crushed all sounds of horses and water, Heriot sang softly and interminably to himself.

Then the stream took a bend and widened into another pool between cliffs vaster and more silent than those the men had passed. There Justin pulled up, Heriot following him. A stone, kicked from Albert Creek's hoof, rolled and dropped with a sound that the cliffs threw back as a gunshot.

'We better camp here,' Justin said, half-whispering for fear of the echo, 'it going to rain pretty soon. We stay dry here.'

Very slowly Heriot dismounted, and went and sat down under the overhang of the rock. There was a flutter of sound as bats burst from some cranny behind him and skittered out across the grey water. He did not move, he sat quietly in the dirt, his arms folded round the rifle.

Justin came over and dumped his blankets and bags, went back and unsaddled. Heriot said nothing, had no direction to give, was willing to be managed by Justin for the rest of his life. He watched the broad face of the man bent over his bundles.

'I brought hopples, too,' Justin said proudly. 'Out of you office.' He held up the hobble chains and jingled them.

'Good,' Heriot murmured.

The white teeth grinned, and the man rose and went to the horses, leading them down to the edge of the water where there was a bank of silt. When he came back Heriot had not moved, still held the rifle clutched to his chest. 'You like you tucker now, brother?' he asked.

'No,' Heriot said, wearily. 'I'm not hungry.'

'I make a fire and we have a cup of tea, eh?'

'If you like.'

He watched the dark figure gathering wood and piling it, and tossed his box of matches when Justin's hands demanded. As the wood crackled, the light came like an explosion, hurting his eyes, so that he turned and looked at the flame-washed rock behind him, patterned with the ochre and charcoal drawings of natives. He saw rock wallabies, crocodiles, goannas, little priapic men. Recurrent everywhere was the symbol of *lumiri*, the rainbow serpent.

'Is this place sacred?' he asked dully.

'No. Plenty old people camp here. Women, too.'

'*Lumiri* can take you to the sky, is that right?'

'Might be,' Justin said noncommittally, crouched over his fire.

Heriot stood up, spread out his blanket and lay down on it, the rifle beside him, He whistled two notes, and the cliffs threw them back clear and pure. He executed a brief phrase and received it back again. With a kind of desperate concentration he applied himself, to composing a duet for his whistle and the echo, involving a pleasant use of counterpoint.

Later, when the quart-pot boiled, he sat propped on one elbow and drank tea, and then lay down again by his rifle. Justin came and spread his blanket and lay beside him, listening to the white man's slow breathing. At last he said: 'Brother?'

'Yes?'

'I take that gun away if you sleepy.'

'No. Leave it.'

'Brother —'

'Yes?'

'You going to say prayer?'

A strange tearing noise came back from the cliffs. The horses, down at the edge of the dark water, were drinking.

'I know a prayer,' Heriot said into his blanket. 'A very old prayer.' He whispered it to the ground.

> 'Fittingly is now my coming
> Into this world with tears and cry;
> Little and poor is my having,
> Brittle and soon y-fallen from high;
> Sharp and strong is my dying,
> I ne wot whither shall I;
> Foul and stinking is my rotting —
> On me, Jesu, thou have mercy.'

The rain shattered on the roof with tireless tropical zeal, eager to have the job done and over, violently intent. If it could deliver three inches in an hour or two, that would be raining, it could rest then until the morning.

Dixon, rising wet and gasping from the darkness like a fish, fetched up at the hospital door and leaned in, looking for Helen, who was marooned on an island of lamplight in a dark room. In the shadow, vaguely, he could see the humped whiteness of Rex's bed. She had put out the electric light and sat removed from him, reading from a solid blue book.

'Helen,' he whispered to her.

She looked up, not seeing him at first, then came quietly out with her book to the veranda. The iron roof roared with rain.

'Is something wrong, Terry?'

'No — least, I hope not. You seen Heriot?'

'Not all day.'

'I took your telegram over there to send to the doctor, but it was too late for the sched, and the old man wasn't there. I felt the wireless and it was cold. I don't think he listened in.'

'Is it working?'

'I'll check up later. The thing is, he wasn't at church either. Ways haven't seen him, nor's anyone else, and when I went over to his house his bed had been pulled to bits and the blankets taken. Looked like he'd shot through.'

She was deeply silent. 'Well,' he asked, 'aren't you surprised?'

'Terry — I don't know anything.'

'Where would he go, on a day like this? Any day, come to that.'

'I don't know,' she said.

'Aren't you scared he might have been knocked down by something, like Rex was? I am.'

She was clutching her book unhappily to herself as Gunn came leaping and dripping on to the veranda. 'The Wet's over,' he said bitterly. 'Get an eyeful of the Dry.'

'You seen Heriot?' Dixon asked.

Gunn shook his head with a shower of drops, and the silence came down on them again. 'Come into the dispensary,' Helen said, to break it.

The yellow-lit room was airless, a feeling of damp lay on chairs and table and skin, and moths were mad with light. 'Better out there, really,' Gunn said.

Dixon wiped his face. 'Well, what are we going to do about the old man? Can't just forget about him.'

Gunn said: 'You knew he'd gone, didn't you, Helen?'

'Yes, I went to his office, and then to his house. I noticed the same things Terry noticed.'

'Anything else? You're probably more observant than we are.'

She hesitated. 'Yes,' she said finally. 'The top rifle from the rack in the office was gone. It's always been there. Always.'

Dixon's puzzled eyes went from her to Gunn, who had stiffened in his chair. 'What is all this?' he asked loudly. 'What's the secret?'

Gunn said quietly and quickly: 'Just a minute, Terry, we're working things out. You cleaned the wound, Helen. The one on the forehead.'

'Yes.'

'What was it like?'

'Ragged,' she said. 'Fairly deep.'

Dixon shifted impatiently. 'So what?'

'It wasn't the iron,' Gunn said. 'Couldn't have been. It didn't look right to begin with. If the wind was strong enough to carry it on so far after hitting him it would have carried it over his head in the first place. And the wound didn't look right either, as far as you could see it. If the iron had hit him flat on you'd expect his nose to be broken and not so much blood on the forehead. And if it had hit him with a corner or edge — well, God knows what it would have done, but it would have been worse than it was.'

'It was a stone,' Helen said flatly. 'I'm sure of it.'

Dixon said abruptly: 'I get what you mean.'

They turned to him, astonished by the change in his voice, his face. No longer an awkward, good-natured man to whom it was not necessary to pay attention, he had hardened and grown and taken on an air of sardonic decision.

Helen said: 'But we don't *know*, Terry....'

'You've got no doubts about it. That old — he tried to kill Rex and then went out and shot himself.'

'We can't be sure,' Gunn protested. 'We could be wrong about the wound.'

'Just because he hated Rex.'

'He was a good man,' Helen said sharply.

'Ah, a good man, all right. At least he knew what he ought to get for it.'

Over the sound of rain: 'Terry,' Helen cried out, 'you must listen to us. He wasn't a bad man. If he tried to kill Rex, it wouldn't have been because he hated him, it would have been because he thought the mission was in danger from him.'

'He might have kidded himself.'

'Terry, you believe in God.'

'Yeah.'

'If you could bring people back from death, would you refuse?'

He looked at her with his farseeing eyes. 'No.'

'We've saved Rex. But I can't save Mr Heriot, you and Bob are the only ones who can do that.'

'Not if he's shot himself.'

'But he took blankets, he can't have meant to do it straightaway, if he meant it at all. There's always a chance, Terry —'

'But he tried to kill someone. He doesn't deserve being saved.'

She had the thick medical book held tightly in her lap, and her voice went on, quickly and passionately in the stifling room: 'I don't believe in heaven and hell, but I believe in sin, and sins that aren't wiped out on the earth stay on the earth forever echoing and echoing among the people left behind. We're trying to wipe out the sin of the white men who massacred these people's relations, but we can't ever quite do it, because we're not the same white men. And Mr Heriot has to come back, he's the only one who can wipe out his hatred of Rex. They'll come to see that as hating and rejecting all of them.'

She stopped then, looking down at her hands, and Gunn broke in quietly. 'We drive people to it,' he said. 'The white men at the massacre thought they were protecting property, and Mr Heriot thought he was protecting the mission. Things we asked them to protect. We can pay reparations to people we hurt in our wars, but we don't ever quite pay back the people we force to hurt them. But with Heriot we can try, Terry, or I will. All you need to do is keep quiet about it, now you know everything.'

Dixon rubbed his hands on his knees, his head bent. 'You can talk,' he said. 'Both of you.'

'Two people have killed one another,' Helen said, 'but we have this chance to bring them back and reconcile them. That's heaven. But if we fail, their hate will go on spreading and growing forever, and that's hell, Terry.'

'I believe you,' he said at last. 'What do you want me to do?'

'Don't let anyone know about Rex, let them think it was the iron. No one else will see the wound.'

'Aren't you going to get the doctor plane for him?'

'He's out of danger, and the airstrip's unserviceable. It'll be a marsh after this rain.'

'How do we stop Father Way from working out why Heriot's shot off?'

'They had a quarrel this morning, Mrs Way told me a little bit she heard of it from him. It'd be easy for me to convince him Mr Heriot was on the verge of suicide.'

'And where do we look for him?' Dixon asked.

Gunn said: 'I'd pick Onmalmeri.'

'Where the ghosts are?'

'He often said he thought it was beautiful, and how he wished he had a few days to ride out and camp there.'

Helen said softly: 'He once told me he'd like to be buried at Onmalmeri. He loathed the cemetery here.'

'I'll go there,' Dixon said. 'One last thing — what about Rex?'

'Helen will talk to him,' Gunn muttered restlessly.

Helen stood up and went to the table and laid her book down there. 'I might as well tell you,' she said, leaning over it, her back to them, 'what I'm going to do.'

'Well, tell us.'

'I don't know if you've thought of it, but Rex, when he wakes up, probably won't remember anything. Retroactive amnesia.'

She felt their faint movements of relief and surprise.

'Well,' said Dixon, 'that'd be a break. That'd be apples, that would.'

'But I'd tell him,' she said.

5

Way said: 'I still find it incredible. Utterly.'

'He wasn't well,' Helen said. She was tired, and sat hugging her knees on the edge of his veranda, with the drowsy scent of frangipani close above her head. 'I've been afraid of — not this, exactly, but some sort of breakdown. I think we're right to fear — well, the worst.'

In his jungle-garden finches haunted the dark green of the poincianas, the frangipanis, the creepers, fluttering restless as butterflies round the dripping leaves. 'But to take Justin . . . .'

'I don't know why he should have done that. It's all much more puzzling now than it was last night, before we knew Justin had gone. But it's more hopeful, if there's someone with him.'

'Of course, there's not much chance of finding tracks, after this wind and rain. Why do you feel so certain he went to Onmalmeri?'

'I don't feel certain, father. But he often said he loved the place, and it had — associations. You remember?' she asked, unable to add, since he knew so little: It is where the murdered people are, the murdered.

Mrs Way, cradled by a deck-chair in the tendrilled shade of her veranda, clicked with her morning tea-cup. 'Poor Mr Heriot,' she said sadly. She was a lean, grey Englishwoman, kindly and calm.

Helen said to the garden: 'It needn't be too late, it needn't. Don't you believe Terry will find him?'

'I only hope,' Mrs Way confessed. 'This country — so vast . . .'

'He *must* be at Onmalmeri. If he isn't, Terry will have wasted nearly two days. If only Justin had told someone —'

'He didn't,' Way said. 'Ella and Stephen can't remember when exactly he left the house. But he took his spears some time before going away, so it sounds as though he meant to make a long trip.'

'You didn't tell me that, dear,' said Mrs Way. 'Now I feel much more optimistic. Perhaps Mr Heriot, not being quite — stable, thought a long journey through the bush would be good for him.'

'We can't be sure of anything, of course. That's why I don't want to report his disappearance until we've done as much as we can to find him. But I'll have to, if he's not at Onmalmeri. He could hardly object, even if he chose to be lost — with two of the best of our wretched little handful of horses, incidentally.'

'I don't think you need be cross with him yet,' Helen said quietly.

'I'm sorry, Helen. I still find the whole thing hard to believe.'

Across the road Harris clanked a few notes on the bell, bringing Helen to her feet. 'Thank you, Mrs Way. I must go to the store, and then back to Rex.'

'Are you pleased with him, Helen?'

'Oh, yes, fairly. It will take time.'

'Such bad luck he has, poor man. First his wife, and now this.'

'Yes,' Helen said, 'very bad luck. But he'll survive this, with that hard head of his. I must go.'

Inside the store Harris, free of customers and glad to talk to someone, stood rolling a cigarette. He looked up and smiled at her with his old, dry face. 'Out of smokes?'

'Yes,' she said. 'Can you see me craving?'

He reached for a packet and entered it in his book. 'I reckon you smoke more than you earn. Should roll 'em.'

'I think I will from now on.'

'Three and a half inches we've had. That's raining.'

'But it seems to be over,' she said, looking through the door at the bright sunlight. 'I hate it like this, just after the sun comes out.'

'It's sticky, all right.'

'Harry,' she asked, lighting a cigarette, 'what do you think about this — about Mr Heriot? We never hear your opinion of anything.'

He had his spidery elbows on the counter and his chin in his hands, staring outside. 'I don't know. I'm just wondering, like everyone.'

'Do you think he would — well, kill himself?'

'Might. You hear of that sort of thing happening.'

'What, here?'

'Well, there was one, not on the staff, but doing a job here. Good few years ago. You take an old man like Heriot, just going to leave the place and not knowing anywhere else much — he might do it.'

'But having Justin with him — wouldn't that stop him?'

'No. If he asked Justin to come with him, that'd mean he wasn't up to anything, but if Justin went after him to bring him back he'd do what he was going to do and tell Justin to get out of the way. It'd annoy him, being followed like that.'

'You're very resigned,' she said hopelessly. 'I couldn't be.' Like him she stared out at the warm, damp sunlight towards which the smoke from their cigarettes was slowly tending, climbing up and out in peaceful ripples. 'But Terry will be at Onmalmeri late this afternoon, and he will be there, Harry, he must be.'

It was mid-afternoon when Dixon arrived at Onmalmeri. After the long day's ride over rocky hills, through man-high canegrass studded with little broad-leaved trees, the *gan*, the wild orange, the wild kapok; after the river flowing shallowly over rock and the ascent to new hills from which one looked down on islands of dense pandanus and cliffs burning red in the light or dull in shadow; after great distances of earth bared by old fires, and sudden cool clumps of gums, and the inescapable rock in boulders and floors and cliffs, he came on a new river, and across the river the cliff of Onmalmeri thrust up from its dark pool.

There was a bird which he had never seen but which he hated savagely, it was there now in the trees or hidden in the pandanus, making its sound like a baby's crying and answering itself with a madwoman's laugh.

Stephen and Gregory were with him and followed him when he dismounted and went down to the water. He lay on his stomach over a flat rock and drank, and sat up again and looked across the pool at the cliff. Galleries ran along it at water level, but above, it was a vast crumbling wall, crazily built of square chunks of rock, coming out in sudden corners edged with red light or bending away into shadow. Pandanus grew at water level in one of its inlets, bright green against the red rock, and trees and spinifex sprouted from its high crannies, or at its top, hundreds of feet above, stretched out against the sky. From across the shadowy pool came to him the low, slow lap of water and a sudden crack of sound as two rock pigeons burst from their shelter far above.

'We'll have to go on foot,' he said, 'up and down the pool and all around, looking for them.'

'More better, brother.'

'You go that way, Gregory. It won't take you long. Fix up the horses and make us a cup of tea for when we get back, it'll take us a while.'

'I do that,' Gregory said.

Dixon stood up. He would have liked to stay longer in that green coolness under the rustling pandanus, but he said: 'Come on, Stephen,' and began rapidly walking away, pushing through the densely growing trees, tearing aside curtains of creeper. The insane bird persevered with its hysterics somewhere among leaves.

Stephen said, quietly thrusting after the white man: 'Might be you better yell out, brother.'

'You do the yelling. You blokes know how to make yourself heard.'

The brown man stopped and shouted: '*Bau!*' through his cupped hands, and waited, but there was only the echo returning, muffled by trees, from the cliff. He shouted again.

'Leave it,' Dixon said, ploughing on. 'We'll go farther.'

So they continued, crawling under bowed trees, avoiding saw-toothed pandanus leaves, breaking through creepers and through low wattles, and came finally past the pool to where there were only rocks, round boulders worn by water and smooth under boot-leather, with clumps of spinifex growing between.

'Any use going on?' Dixon asked.

'There one more pool, brother.'

Dixon took off his hat and wiped his forehead. 'You lead the way,' he said.

Walking behind the native he felt, suddenly, regret at his own awkwardness, for Stephen moved over the rocks with the sureness of a bird, but he stumbled and slipped, having always to plan his next step, to tread carefully. He saw himself for the first time as a stranger, cast without preparation into a landscape of prehistory, foreign to the earth. Only the brown man belonged in this wild and towering world.

'What do you think about all this, Steve?' he asked abruptly.

'What that, brother?'

'Heriot sort of adopted you, didn't he? And isn't Justin your cousin's husband?'

'Yes.'

'You must be wondering what's happened to them.'

'They reckon they come out camping and get lost,' Stephen said.

That was Way's thin story, and he was pretending to believe it. Dixon grinned wryly, picking his way along behind.

The stones gave place to earth and canegrass and they arrived among trees again, before a little pool so sheltered by cliffs that lilies still floated delicately on its water, untouched by the late wind and rain. The cliff opposite had been split in halves by a landslide, and a huge passageway littered with boulders ran up through it, ending in a rock wall and the sky. The enormous chunks of rock thrown down in the ruin stuck up sharply at the pool's edge, or rose out of it like islands, and from among them, twisted and tortuous, a wild fig tree thrust out its branches of dark, shining leaves towards the water.

Stephen said: 'Brother — some people reckon Brother Heriot went to finish off himself.'

Dixon stared at the cliff. 'It might be true. Sorry, but you ought to know what's going on.'

The world was utterly silent. 'Brother, why he do that?'

'I don't know, Steve.'

'I thinking — I thinking might be he do it — because of me, brother.'

'Ah, come off it.'

'Because — I'm no good, I'm thief, no good. And my sister — you know? That why I think that, brother.'

'You're up the pole,' Dixon muttered uneasily. 'Just help me find him, don't worry about yourself.'

'I going to help you, brother. That old man, he just like my father to me.'

'Well, give him another shout, then.'

The man cupped his brown hands to his mouth and shouted: '*Bau!*' over the water, and got it back again as a far, desolate echo. 'Nothing,' he said, in an empty voice.

'Let's go back.'

'I coming, brother.'

Returning over the stones, looking at the high rocky hillside between the two pools: 'You could climb up there,' Dixon said. 'You could look down over the whole place. You coming?'

Stephen nodded, they moved across the stones to the hill, climbing up steps of rock and up the rock bed of a vanished creek and among red boulders in canegrass. Dixon panted, swore involuntarily when he slipped on canegrass stems flattened over rock. Stephen showed tender concern.

Coming finally to the top of the hill, where meagre gums grew from rock, they stopped for breath before tramping on to the cliff. A wind had come up across country, stirring the leaves and the tall grass. Dixon opened his shirt and felt it cool on his sweating chest.

At the edge of the cliff, on an overhang above the water the country filled his eyes, beauty struck at him, and in a strange stillness of mind he recognized it. He looked at a land of rock, a broad valley between cliffs and hills, even the floor of it studded with broken stone. But the pools were bright blue under the sky, and the endless hills blue also. In some places the water was almost obliterated by lily-leaves and grass, in others fringed with dense trees and pandanus. Below him, many miles down, he thought, lay the Onmalmeri pool, shrunken by distance, dark, dark green among its thickets of wattle and pandanus, its creeper-choked gums. He picked up a stone and threw it far out, and it swerved and landed with an echoing clatter in the clump of pandanus at the cliff foot. A cry of birds broke out.

On the far bank, beside the smoke of his fire, a tiny man, Gregory, looked across at the noise. The toy horses started and stared.

What am I thinking? Dixon asked himself. But it'd be easy to give up here, to get out on an overhang and drop into the water. That'd be a death to die, you could easily do that, with the water just about calling you on. Wonder if those little crocs would eat a dead man, they don't touch live ones.

Gregory had seen them and called out, his voice rising, magnified by echo, so that it seemed impossible such sound should come from so small a figure.

'*Bau!*' shouted Stephen over the empty country. '*Bau! Bau!*'

But there was no answer beyond echo, and presently Gregory called: 'Nothing?'

'Nothing,' Dixon repeated. The lonely echo threw up in its broken voice: 'Nothing.'

In the narrow gorge, sunset firing the farther cliffs, Heriot sang to himself, under his roof of rock, songs of loneliness and silence.

Presently he himself lapsed into silence, listening to the rapids downstream, watching the shadow slowly creep up the cliffs. His blanket smelt of acrid woodsmoke, and his clothes, and his skin, an annoyance that

Justin did not notice, being inured to sleeping all night in the stink of burning cadjiput branches.

'I should have gone to Onmalmeri,' he said. 'I wouldn't feel so closed in there.'

'No, brother,' Justin said automatically. He sat, idle and bored, propped against the cliff base, on a rock beside a few bream which he had speared in the pool with his prong-wire.

'We'll go on, we'll go tomorrow.'

'Yes, brother.'

'*Le silence éternel de ces espaces infinis m'effraie.*'

'Yes, brother.'

'You're not listening,' Heriot said bitterly.

'I were thinking, brother.'

'We'll go on, as soon as the sun gets up, tomorrow.'

'Yes.'

Four brolgas, attenuated and grey, crossed the sky with a long purring crake like the opening of an old door. Heriot sat up.

'What are you thinking?' he demanded.

'Nothing.'

'Damn you,' said Heriot.

'What that, brother?'

'Damn you, damn you, damn you,' whispered Heriot to the sky. 'You do me wrong, you do me wrong to take me out of the grave.'

When the fire had died down, Dixon in his sleep became vaguely conscious of the absence of light on his eyelids, and woke, and threw more wood on it. It crackled, then bloomed into flame. The great flame of fire, he thought, remembering Justin's voice. The light in its first blaze leaped to the edge of the water, then darkness pushed it back.

One of the blanketed sleepers stirred. 'That good, brother.'

'You awake, Gregory?'

'Little bit.'

'Not scared of the ghosts?'

'No, I not scared. But I don't like sleeping in this place, brother.'

Crawling back to his blanket: 'I don't go much on it, either,' Dixon confessed.

He lay still. Far away up the valley a dingo howled, and howled again, lonely, forsaken.

But that's not it, he thought. He drifted into sleep again and dreamed of a dark woman with her child, and he was full of grief. Don't do that, he said, don't cry. But she was bent over her child. *Wawai! wawai! wawai!* she crooned, rocking the baby to sleep.

In the morning Heriot woke happy, light filled the gorge and reached his bones, he felt careless and at ease. Justin, at the fire, grilling his fish, looked up warily and saw the old man's face, and smiled, whitely and warmly. 'You feeling good again,' he said.

'Very good,' said Heriot, squatting beside him. 'Ah, you're a good man, Justin, you even brought salt.'

'Those horses pretty glad we going,' Justin said, jerking his head towards the impatient Albert Creek. 'Look 'im, eh, real hungry for grass.'

'I'll go for a swim,' said Heriot restlessly. 'I'll be clean.' He walked briskly down to the sand and the water, and he was upright and strong. When he had dragged off his clothes he considered his body and thought that it was younger than his mind.

Across the fire Justin watched him enter the water, balancing cautiously on the slimy sunken rocks, his body white as a tree-trunk but with dark-brown forearms and neck that did not seem to belong to it. A trace of compassion touched the dark man's thick mouth as he applied himself to his cooking.

When Heriot came out of the water his hair was flattened in strips over his forehead and drops hung in the white stubble on his face. He dried himself perfunctorily on his shirt, and dressed. His clothes stank, he discovered, but was not distressed. He went back to the fire and found Justin had finished his preparations; there was a billy full of tea and the fish was good, fine and juicy. 'Ah, you're a good man,' Heriot threw out vaguely.

When he had eaten he pulled out his tobacco tin, looked in, frowning uncertainly, then closed it again and gazed into the fire.

'I got cigarette if you wanting one,' Justin offered.

'I've got some,' said Heriot, 'but I should save it. Matches, too. Oh, what does it matter?' demanded Heriot of himself. 'When it's gone, it's gone.' He opened the tin again and rolled a cigarette.

Justin asked diffidently: 'How far we going, brother?'

Lighting his cigarette at the fire, puffing smoke: 'I don't know,' Heriot replied.

'Brother —'

'Well?'

'I know why you come out here. That why I followed you. I knew.'

'What?' asked Heriot. 'What did you know?'

Justin said softly: 'You were going to — going to kill youself, brother, with that gun.'

Heriot sat unmoving in front of the fire, his back to Justin: 'How did you know?'

'It all over you face, brother. And that gun in you hand — I knew.'

'Justin,' said Heriot harshly, 'Justin, you should have left me alone.'

'I couldn't do that, brother. Following you, that was only thing I could do. If,' Justin said, with a protest in his voice, 'if you was black fellow, I could take that gun and say: "You don't do that, go home now." But you can't say that to white man, you can't do nothing, only follow.'

'I don't want to die,' said Heriot, pleading with someone. 'Not today.'

'Come back to mission. Please, brother.'

'I can't go back.'

'You saying you don't want to die.'

'Justin,' said Heriot. 'You don't know what I've done.'

He turned, and the look on the craggy face silenced Justin.

'Rex is dead, he was dead when you left, lying outside in the wind. I killed him, Justin. Now I have to die.'

Smoke from the fire drifted between them as they watched one another.

'It's no good your following me, I can't ever go back. But I want to live now, as long as I can. I want to go on and on. And I'm afraid to — do justice to myself. I can only — give myself to the country, and let it do what it likes with me. That would be God's justice.'

'Maybe Rex not dead,' Justin said unsteadily. 'Sister Bond, she real clever, she fix him —'

'Can't you see, it doesn't matter if he's dead or not. All that matters is that I wanted him dead. But he died. I know. Sister Bond can't raise Lazarus.'

With a sudden movement of despair Justin reached for the rifle and pulled it across his knees, slipping the safety catch. 'Brother,' he said thickly, 'I sorry, but you got to come back.'

'Oh, Justin,' said Heriot, softly, smiling, 'if I believed you'd shoot me, I'd kiss your feet.'

The brown man was baffled by his sincerity, he laid the rifle down on the ground. And Heriot, reaching out, seized it.

'This is a ridiculous charade,' he said, sourly grinning, 'but I have to make you go back. I'm going nowhere. Ella and your children need you and you need them.'

'I can't go back!' Justin protested, with bewilderment and anger. 'If I go back, what they going to say? They going to say I let the man what murdered Rex go away, and they going to say I let Brother Heriot kill himself, and they going to say I was scared to know what to do. Ella and my little kids going to say the same, brother.'

'No one will blame you. They know I killed Rex, and they know I can't live in this country.'

'Might be Rex not dead. Then it would be like I kill you, brother.'

'Go home,' Heriot said.

'I never going home, brother. You can't stop me following you, only if you shoot me. I know what right, I not leaving you.'

'I see,' Heriot whispered. He began to tremble, a nerve twitched near his mouth and his tongue was stiff with nausea. 'There's only one thing I can do.'

As he stood up Justin leapt at him and seized the rifle, and they struggled for it, thigh to thigh, in absolute silence, the black man and the white, with the murmur of water drifting up from below the pool and the horses restlessly watching from the sandbank. When the shot came, the cliffs took it and threw it back and forwards between them like a sharp, close crack of thunder, and the men froze. Then Justin stepped back, holding the rifle.

Heriot swung away and went to his horse, and saddled up, Justin all the time silently watching. He led it to the rock shelves, and mounted, and rode on.

When he had gathered up blankets and bags Justin followed and overtook him. And all morning they climbed in silence through the ranges, among rocky hills capped and feathered with grey-green cypress pine, and at noon they came out on a broad tableland and a thicket of saplings through which the horses pushed and strained irritably.

Green budgerigars shrilled through the air, and there appeared briefly two blue parrots, crimson underwings glowing against the sky.

In the silence after their going Heriot sang.

Gunn was with Way in the office when Dixon came back, and both turned quickly to hear him as he appeared at the door. But he only shook his head, hot and weary after the long ride, and sat down on the step.

The room sweated in the afternoon sun. 'So it's no good.' Way said. 'He wasn't there.'

'No.'

'I'd better tell you, Terry, about the telegrams.'

'What telegrams?'

'Two came from the council today, one for Heriot, one for me. Here they are, if you can read my writing.' He passed into Dixon's reaching hand a sheet from the pad beside the wireless, and waited. Dixon's mouth formed the words as he read.

'Well,' he said finally, 'that puts us right. No doubt about it now.'

He pushed the sheet of paper back across the table and it lay there, by Gunn's hand, with its messages pencil-scrawled by Way. *Heriot. Telegram 21 March received resignation reluctantly accepted many regrets good wishes. Way. Please accept position acting superintendent as Heriot arranges.*

'There you are,' Way said.

'What do we do now?'

'I think we report it. The telegrams should be enough justification. If he resigned on the morning he disappeared it's pretty clear what he meant to do.'

'And then what happens? Search plane go over?'

'Probably.'

'You beaut. Wait till the money starts rolling in. Stories in the paper. "Man lost in rugged country." Old ladies and gents remembering there's a mission here and shaking up the moneybags.'

'We mustn't be mercenary,' Way said, in a disciplined voice. 'Not yet.'

'I don't believe in it now,' Dixon confessed. His eyes were full of huge landscapes, it was hard to be concerned with the fate of one ant-like man.

'I have to remind myself now and then. It seems as though he's been gone for years.'

Gunn said: 'What good would a plane do? It wouldn't pick out men on horses, except maybe if they were moving across open plain. You'll need a land party.'

'But how're you going to know which way to go?' Dixon demanded, 'unless a plane goes over and spies out the most likely way they'd have taken.'

'I want to go and look for him. Starting tomorrow.'

'You can't go,' Way said firmly. 'You've got the school. You can't leave that.'

'Helen could take it. The Education Department needn't know.'

'You can't go,' Way said decisively.

'Have to be my job, anyway,' Dixon added. 'Forget it, Bob.'

'Ah, kick me, spit on me,' Gunn said, 'roll me in the dirt. All right, I'm no use.'

Way said: 'No insult, but leave the dirty work to your tribal elders. We'll struggle through.'

'Well, I hope Mr Heriot'll struggle through. Do you think he'll be out there waving his little white hanky when the plane goes over?'

There was a silence, and then they began to laugh, all three of them, without any reason except that they felt tired and puzzled and none of them had been quite listening to the others. 'Ah, heck,' Dixon said at last, 'it's not funny, but you've got to laugh, I don't know.'

'Aren't we cheerful?' Way remarked. 'Funny thing.'

Dixon got up slowly and stretched himself. 'Heriot not being here,' he said, 'that makes the difference.' He scratched himself and made monkey noises. 'I feel drunker than I've felt since I was drunk.'

'Could you sober up enough to take the launch in tonight?' Way wondered.

'I reckon.'

Gunn said suddenly: 'He's going to die. That old man's going to die. We make me sick.' They looked at each other in the hot little room with faces blank as stone.

Coming down the hillside, seeing, instead of rock, spreading grasslands patched here and there with blue pools and with gum trees, cadjiputs, and lonely baobabs, Heriot sighed and felt peace rise like a wind from the plain. The horses struggled down the slope, but at the bottom was a clump of pandanus, and a shock of cool air heavy with the smell of damp grass, so that they revived, nervously, and remembered that there were other things in the world beyond stones and heat.

'That pool,' said Heriot, 'that waterhole, that looks fine, that looks like a pool to bring a man back to life.'

'Yes,' Justin said.

They made towards it, the sun in their eyes, hanging low over the flat-peaked blue hills to the far west with their high diadems of rock. 'We have far to go,' Heriot said. 'But here's a pretty place for bed and a bath.'

'You stop here,' Justin said, pulling up and slipping out of the saddle. 'I going to get duck.' He made off towards the pool, bent low, looking apelike with the rifle hanging from one long arm.

Heriot sang to himself peacefully. Presently there was a shot, and a clatter of wings as cloud upon cloud of ducks rose in relays from the water and streamed overhead with a high ethereal whistling, as if some stringed instrument had been hurled with great force through the air. Heriot waited, knowing their habit, until the flock turned, far away across the plain, and came whistling back over the pool and wheeled again, and finally, with a volley of splashes, descended on the water. Then there was briefly silence, before the second shot came and the birds took to air again, whistling and wheeling distressfully over the grassland. From the pool Justin shouted.

When Heriot came to the water's edge, leading Justin's horse, the brown man was wading out of the water, and stood proud and naked among the lilies holding in each hand a limp duck. The low sunlight glowed through lily petals as if through quartz, and Justin stood in a circle of ripples ridged with light.

'Hawk-eyed hunter,' Heriot said courteously. 'That, with a rifle, is clever.'

'You get off and sit down,' Justin said. 'You looking real tired.'

But Heriot sat still in his saddle, watching the sun with red-veined eyes. His wild hair glowed with light at the edges, there were lights also in the white stubble on his face.

His back ached, he ached all over from riding. He closed his eyes.

'Old man —'

'What?'

'Don't you go to sleep, sitting up there.'

'I'm not sleepy,' Heriot said. 'I'm in love. Never say good-bye. This earth seduces me.'

'Get down, old man.'

'I grudge stopping. I'm thirsty for horizons.'

'Look 'im, eh,' Justin said, with a deep eruption of laughter. 'Real sleepy now, like little kid.'

'Are you afraid, Justin?'

'Me? No, I not afraid.'

'Come on with me. There's nothing in the past, there's nobody behind us or ahead. Doomsday will find us.'

'I coming with you,' Justin promised. He threw his ducks in the grass, reached for Albert Creek's bridle and led him away towards the single baobab that stood guard over the waterhole. 'You get down here,' he said, grinning privately, shining dark and wet in the late sun. 'You go to sleep.'

Heriot turned from the assisting arms and sank down beside the swollen tree trunk. The cool scents of damp grass and reeds and water washed over him, drowned him, he fell asleep.

'And remember Sophy,' Way prayed in the crowded church, 'in the leprosarium at Derby, and Molly and Maurice in hospital at Darwin, and Rex, here, in our own hospital. And remember especially Brother Heriot and Justin, and all others in sickness or distress of mind or body. May God in His mercy guard them, watch over them in all adversity, and bring them at the end to everlasting life.'

In the still church the amen came loud and firm. They love him, Helen thought, now, when he is in trouble. Now they can give the white man what they need most to give but are never allowed, their kindness and their pity. And now I love them, too, they are good people.

On the heels of the organ they swung into singing, and she, singing with them, found in their voices a depth and a sincerity that she had never noticed before, so that she was taken by surprise and felt a stiffness of tears in her throat. The hymn welled up and broke out over the grass half-walls to the hot night and the earth lying dead as the moon under a still sky:

> 'Guide me, O Thou great Redeemer,
> Pilgrim through this barren land;
> I am weak, but Thou art mighty,
> Hold me with Thy powerful hand;
> > Bread of Heaven,
> > Bread of Heaven,
> Feed me now and evermore,
> Feed me now and evermore.'

At first the boat sat, white with moonlight, on mud. Then the tide began to creep in, circling through mud channels, until it reached the soft island in mid-stream and the boat listed and floated and rose on the brown water. On the mud-bank below the cliff the mangroves stood deep in the currents of the twice-a-day river.

Afterwards, a dinghy put out from the shadow of a baobab on the near bank and one of the dark figures in it boarded the boat. The lights went on, and out again, the engine roared. Presently the boat moved up the water, and turning came gradually in to the landing-stage and to silence.

Way, standing in the shadow of the baobab, pulled an envelope from his pocket and said: 'Don't let me forget this, Terry. It's the report you have to make to the police.'

'Let's have a look at it,' Dixon said, taking it out and reading it over in the light of Way's torch. ' "Miss Bond, the nurse," ' he mumbled, ' "confirms that Mr Heriot had been in a depressed state of mind for some time, a fact which had been obvious to many of us. We therefore think there is good reason to fear that his motive in disappearing may have been to inflict injury on himself." I couldn't say that to Bill Williams,' he protested. 'He'd bust himself laughing.'

'Well, put it in your own words and then give them the statement.'

The men were standing waiting on the lighted boat. 'Time we pushed off,' Dixon said. 'See you, padre.' He stuffed the envelope into his shirt pocket and went on board.

The boat drifted out from the landing-stage into mid-river. Then the lights went out, the engine roared, the light of Way's torch under the trees receded and disappeared. They travelled for three hours among mud-banks thicketed with mangroves, past cliffs rising sheer out of the water and rocky hills softened a little by trees. At the mouth of the river they anchored for the turning of the tide, and there the slack water mirrored the Southern Cross, and the sudden flash of a torch picked out red eyes of crocodiles among the mangroves. After sleeping briefly they took to the sea, and came in the early morning in sight of the little township cowering under its mountains, where the hawks wheeled and watched forever over their high, vertical country.

6

Heriot woke to the harsh outcry of crows, it was a crow his eyes saw first as they opened unwillingly on the light of day. A shining bird, it clung in the tree close above his head and broadcast its discovery to the air. Presently two more crows came planing in to join it and to perch and peer sidelong at the prone man.

'You think I'm dead,' he said. 'Damn your impudence. I'm a strong man yet.' He got to his feet energetically and waved his blanket at them, so that they flew, protesting.

Justin was in his usual post at the fire, smoke rising blue and clear into the sky. 'I'll never starve,' Heriot said, coming up behind him, 'while I have you.'

The brown man looked round with a grin. 'I thinking we better keep that tin food. Not much there, old man. You like duck?'

'*Jau, ngaia nambal.*' He took the little cooked wing Justin handed to him and chewed it.

'Good, eh?'

'*Manambara.*'

'Why you talking language now, old man? *Angundja-gu jei gram?*'

'*Gadea gabu,*' Heriot said, '*ngaia bendjin, nawuru morong nangga.* No more white man. I'm a blackfellow, son of the sun.'

Justin laughed, slow and shy, looking up glowingly from under his jutting forehead. There was grey in his hair, Heriot saw, and it showed in the incipient beard, but his smile was young. '*Maoba,*' he said, 'old man, *bendjin* don't always say *gadea* for white man.'

'No?'

'Most of the people, they say *djuari* or they say *bungama*, because you all white like devil-devil or ghost.'

'*Bungama ngarang,*' said Heriot contentedly. 'I am a ghost.'

'Which way we going today?'

'*Gala.* That way. West. To track the sun.'

'*Gare,*' Justin said, 'okay. Now you have you breakfast.'

When they had packed up and were moving again a troop of hawks came and hovered over their heads and moved with them, hanging so low that Heriot, when he looked up, could see their watching eyes.

'What are they doing?' he asked, suddenly frightened and old.

'They just looking at us. They not cheeky.'

'Why are they following me?'

'They follow anyone, old man.'

'No,' Heriot said shakily, 'they're following me, they're waiting for me to die.' He screamed at the hawks: 'Get away, you filthy vultures, go on! I'm not going to die!' But they wheeled still.

'Don't look at them,' Justin advised, 'they go away soon, they got their own countries.'

'Shoot them,' Heriot commanded. 'Where's the rifle? Give it to me. Why are they watching me?'

'They all right, old man.'

'Filthy birds! Look at them,' Heriot raged, 'watching me. They're going to follow us, all the way. Why don't you shoot them, damn you?'

'They always around,' Justin said. But though the birds presently dropped back, others rose and briefly followed as the two men rode on towards the new range; and when, hours later, they stopped to rest and eat by a palm-shadowed spring at the foot of one of the sentinel hills, the hawks were above, circling the peak in restless vigilance.

'Why is the earth so hungry?' Heriot protested weakly. 'Where is God?'

Standing in the tin shade of one of the stores, bored and out of place, Dixon thought longingly of the mission. Here, in this little shanty township, he was a foreigner. He felt an urge to call out after people he had known in his unregenerate days: 'Hey, look, I'm a human, I don't go round preaching and Bible-bashing, I'm still an ordinary bloke.' But it would have been useless. His acquaintances knew that something strange had happened to Terry Dixon, and if you got too close to him he might start talking about it, and that would be intolerable. So there was unease in their manner when they spoke to him, and no conversation lasted very long.

In the shade of the same store a young English couple were forlornly waiting. Came off the boat, Dixon thought, most likely flew to Darwin and now they're going down the coast, seeing the sights. Good luck to them. The man, looking around him with tired disbelief, said gloomily: 'God, this place doesn't really exist. It's an hallucination of the underprivileged.'

Dixon wandered away and turned at the end of the street towards the foreshore where the brown sea lapped at the brown mud. The sea and the hills hemmed in the town, it could never be more than one street wide. The boat rode at anchor on the water, and he could see one of the boys asleep on the deck, but there was no sign of the others. But he guessed where they would be, and strolled on towards the citadel of empty petrol drums on the shore, and through its passages, walled higher than his head, until a whispered: '*Djuari brambun!*' stopped him. White man, devil-devil coming.

They were sitting in a kind of room inside their labyrinth, and seeing a few scattered cards he knew that they had been playing their own peculiar form of poker with a few natives from the town. The cowboy hat that he remembered seeing on Arthur's head, during the trip in, now sat on a stranger, but Matthew had acquired a girl's scarf and had it knotted round his throat. Around them lay broken and empty beer bottles, relics of ancient parties. But they had not been drinking, they swore it with their defiantly innocent eyes as they watched him.

'When we go, brother?' Matthew asked eventually.

'Tonight's tide. That's what I came to tell you. Should be about ten past eleven if I've worked it out right.'

Arthur gave an exaggerated sigh. 'I happy now, brother. This country make me sick.'

Wish it made you sicker, Dixon thought. Wish it made you sick enough to stay on the boat and leave these town blokes alone. Lines from a song that Gunn sang with the children round the piano came back to him.

> Tell Bill, when he leaves home,
> To let them down-town coons alone.
> This morning. This evening. So soon.

'This isn't our country,' he said. 'The mission's our country.'

'I feeling homesick,' Matthew complained, 'away from my country.'

Dixon grinned. He liked them, he would have preferred to stay with them, but he was more than ever foreign to them, and unwanted, here. He was foreign everywhere, and disliked it, being a friendly man and anxious to be in no way different from the rest of the human race. At such times he recognized, without congratulating or pitying himself, the extent of his sacrifice. But there was no help for it, he could only go and fix up about a few stores, then drift into the hotel and sit about somewhere waiting for the tide. It's a dog's life, he thought. I feel homesick for Matthew's country, too.

Waiting in the still room, oddly nervous: 'You don't remember anything?' Helen asked softly. 'Nothing at all?'

Below the white bandages Rex's eyes were very bright and very lost. 'I don't remember nothing, sister. What happen to me?'

'Wait, Rex, tell me — what was the last thing you remember?'

'I were walking in all that dust. It real windy then. Getting dark, too . . .'

'And then?'

'Nothing,' Rex said, his voice blank as his face. 'Just getting dark.'

She remembered a day in her childhood when she had gone out with a farmhand and met with an accident. It had been clear daylight when they left the house, but as they crossed the paddock darkness began to fall. It was twilight when they reached the gate, and when they passed through it, night. Later in the day she had fallen from a tree and been carried home unconscious, but though they told her afterwards all that had happened she could never remember more than that, the dimness through which she perceived the gate, and the entry into nothing. Now, since it seemed likely that Rex also had lost irrecoverably this small part of his life, she began to see why Dixon and Gunn had so vehemently cried down her proposal to tell him the truth, and was afraid they were right in calling her reckless and irrational. Yet she clung to the conviction that there could be no healing of the wounds inflicted by Heriot unless Rex knew and forgave.

Her fingers were restless, making pleats in her skirt and smoothing them away. 'You don't remember seeing anyone?' she asked hesitantly. 'You don't remember Brother Heriot?'

'No, sister. He weren't there then.'

'Rex — what do you think of Brother Heriot?'

The thick eyebrows lowered a little and the eyes looked away. 'He don't like me, sister.'

'But if he was in trouble, you'd forgive him, wouldn't you, and shake hands?'

The man said suddenly and with bitterness: 'I don't apologize to no one no more. When you apologize, they just think you beaten then. They just laugh at you. I sick of that.'

'I don't mean apologizing, Rex, I mean forgiving. Forgiving someone who has done wrong to you. Wouldn't you do that?'

'Might be, if they was sorry. Brother Heriot, he done wrong to me, but he not sorry. He never sorry, that old man.'

'Rex, listen. Brother Heriot has disappeared. He's gone bush somewhere and he might never come back. He may be dead. Don't you feel sorry for him now?'

After a moment he nodded, but bewilderedly. 'What for he done that, sister?'

Now, she thought, now I'm going to prove myself really a fool. If I left things here I'd have done quite enough. But to keep him in the dark because he doesn't remember would be as unfair as to ignore the whole thing because he's black. And there must be forgiveness, there must be reconciliation, for everyone's sake. And she said, with extreme care: 'You may as well know what happened to you that afternoon.'

'Someone hit me?' he asked listlessly.

'Why, you don't — you don't remember — do you?'

'No, sister. But plenty people,' he said with a faint grin, 'don't like me.'

'Supposing someone had hit you, and you knew — what would you do?'

'Hit him, sister. Real hard.'

'I'll explain to you. You were hit with a stone, and you fell and hurt your head on another stone.'

'Yes, sister? That was woman, eh?'

'Oh, can't you see?' she demanded impatiently. 'I'm trying to tell you that we think Brother Heriot threw the stone. And then, when he thought you were dead, he ran away, and Justin followed him.'

The dark eyes stared at her. He was stricken into silence.

'Well?' she asked. 'Haven't you anything to say?'

'I — I don't know, sister. It real hard for me to believe that.'

'I know it must be, but —'

'Justin gone, too?'

'Yes.'

'Might be Justin try to kill me, and Brother Heriot see him and chase him.'

She had never thought of that possibility, and was suddenly in terror that he might be right, that she had accused Heriot unjustly, that she had done irreparable harm to the mission and to the whole white race. 'But Justin —' she said. 'Justin?'

He began to look even a little pleased with the idea of Heriot's threatening his life. 'That old man, he must hate me a lot,' he said wonderingly.

'No,' she protested, 'not hate you, love you, all of you. It's because he loves you and you disappoint him that he's so bitter and angry. It's because he's given his life to you and you waste it. He's a good man.'

'Where you think he are now, sister?'

'I don't know. None of us knows. He may be dead.'

Rex stared at her.

'He ran away because he thought he'd hurt you. You see, he was so sorry he wanted to die.'

'Yes, sister?'

'So you must forgive him, and pray for him, and never tell anyone what I've told you. And if he comes back you must go up to him and say you're his friend, and he'll be yours, always.'

She watched his face, and in doing so could sense the emotions that were moving him. She felt his incredulity, then an odd sort of pride that hatred of him should have forced a divinity like Heriot to such an action. Then something stronger and stranger, a mixture of fear and humility.

'Sister,' he said, huskily.

'What is it?'

'I know why that old man want me dead. It because — it because he reckon I kill my wife, sister.'

'I know he thought that —'

'He always saying that. He not fair to me!'

'Perhaps not —'

'He say I give her a belting, and then she have that little dead baby and she die then.'

'I know. I've heard what he said.'

He held the sheet clenched tightly in his hands; his voice had gone higher, his mouth and brows were twisted, and she saw with astonishment that he was seized with grief. 'You reckon that true?' he demanded of her. 'Sister, *you* reckon that true?'

They came to a valley in the foothills, the floor covered with broken rocks, the sides cliffs. Thick grass grew up through the rocks, sign of a stream, but the water was overgrown and probably foul and the source not to be seen.

'Might be pool up there,' Justin said, pointing. 'Better we go up there and camp now.'

Heriot said nothing. He was in a daze, tired to the bones, and the stillness racked him like an eternally recurring noise. So lulled, so deadened, he followed Justin without a word as the brown man turned his horse across the valley floor to the smooth shelves of rock at the base of the cliffs.

They rode in a silence relieved only by the rattle of stones from the horses' hoofs. Trees, grass, and water were still as death, and beyond them was nothing but rock. They passed a stretch of rock pitted and wrinkled like lava. How old is this country? Heriot wondered. But it's not old, it's just born, the sea has never been over it, it was created yesterday, dead as the moon. Let the sea some day come up and drown it and fish come swimming out of the rock-pigeons' holes. I will ride with my hair green and wild, through the canyons of the sea.

In the silence there came a sudden irruption of sound, the crackle of fire. They stopped, listening, horses and men frozen like statues against the carved cliffs. Then movement came into the scene with the slow drifting of smoke across the valley from the cliff top.

'There somebody,' Justin whispered. 'There, look. Cane-grass fire.'

Heriot stared blankly.

'Bush people, old man. They seen us.'

'Bless their black hearts,' Heriot said listlessly.

Justin grinned. 'They going to listen to me,' he said. 'I got gun.'

Then there was quiet again except for the fire. Someone was watching them, but who it was or where there was nothing to show. Only the smoke, slowly drifting over.

'We can't go no farther,' Justin said, pointing at the outcrop of cliff ahead of them. 'We got to walk. I fix up horses, eh, and come after you?'

Dismounting, resigning his horse, Heriot began to pick his way painfully along the rock towards the obstruction, all his years and more in the aching spine, the stiff sore legs. He sang to himself in order to forget his pains. Justin caught up with him and supported him as he edged his way round the jutting rock.

Ahead of them the valley ended in cliffs, steeper than any above them, half of the wall in deep shadow, half burning redly in the sun. There was no exit but the way they had come. At the end there was perhaps a pool, but long grass and low trees hid it. Below them the rock shelf dropped steeply down into a little pond choked with grass and lilies.

Justin put his hands to his mouth and shouted: '*Bau!*' Echoes rattled. '*Gui!*' he called. 'Djanama!'

The words lapsed into the same stillness. 'Djanama,' he muttered aside to Heriot, 'that my bush name.'

'What a pretty name,' Heriot said vacantly. 'My name is Arriet.'

'*Gui!*' Justin shouted again. 'Djanama-a-a-a!'

As they moved forward the air came suddenly to life, with the high shouts of women and the bark of dogs under the farther cliffs. Then, between trees, a woman appeared, her incredibly ancient red dress hanging in rags over her shrunken body. She stood, arms drooping crookedly down, watching their approach.

Justin went forward to meet her; and they looked at one another, nervous, distrustful, until he impatiently laid down the blanket roll, foodbag, and rifle with which he had loaded himself and reached out and touched her with both hands. Then she, reluctantly, with her bird-claw fingers did the same.

They struggled to express themselves to one another, both wishing to know the other's country and business, both speaking different languages. But finally some sort of understanding came. Justin turned and called out to Heriot: 'She say she come from that other mission, up that way, but most time all this people live here. She don't talk English. She say this people don't like white man.'

Heriot shrugged.

A man came through the bushes, a tall man wearing tattered khaki shorts, and old, with tangled white hair and beard. He surveyed Heriot suspiciously from under jutting brows, seeming to bear out all the woman had said of her people's hostility. But abruptly, in an astonishing transformation, he grinned, and came forward laughing with shy goodwill to take Heriot's hands.

'Alunggu,' Heriot said in a lost voice. 'So you're alive.'

'*Jau,*' Alunggu confirmed strongly. 'Likem budj; me — budj beoble; me — gamb long budj, all dime now. You — bin — go long budj, now, eh?'

'I old man,' Heriot said. 'Close up dead. I go along bush now, yes.'

'You — gamb — 'ere?'

'I'm running from the hawks. Going to the islands. I camp anywhere.'

Alunggu frowned, half-comprehending. 'Beoble,' he said, 'beoble no — glogj.'

'What do I care for clothes?' Heriot asked of the air. 'I want to sleep. Anywhere.'

Justin spoke in his own language to Alunggu, and the old man reached out for Heriot's hand, leading him on. Past the bushes and the

74

rocks, they came on a camp area, dotted with bough shelters in the shadows of which ancient women and decrepit men sat in weary peace. A small, deep pool lay below the cliffs and was shadowed greenly by pandanus and vine-strangled trees. Everything in the valley existed in a state of suspended life, the trees were still, and the old, naked people sat like water-sculptured stones.

Justin murmured to Alunggu, a small, dry sound. In answer the old man pointed towards the cliff a little back from the edge of the pool and made towards it, leading Heriot behind him. The ancient statues made no move, no sound; a few of them watched the strangers, but most stared rigidly in front of them. Under the overhanging of rock which Alunggu had indicated, the newcomers found a smoothed patch of earth, and there Justin threw down his load.

'We camp here, old man,' he said. 'That all right, eh?'

But Heriot said nothing, being stricken also with the valley's silence. He sat down on the blanket roll and stared. Beside him, Alunggu and Justin took up their murmured conversation again, and presently Justin said: 'This old man want me to go and get kangaroo with my gun. I come back pretty soon. You wait, eh?'

'Yes,' Heriot muttered. 'Yes.'

'I see you later, old man.'

'Yes,' Heriot said feebly.

They went from him then and disappeared, returning to view long afterwards on the top of the cliffs, but he did not see them. For a long time he sat in the petrified attitude of his hosts, until through his trance consciousness came of the clammy discomfort of his clothes and the grime of his body, so that he stood up and went to the pool and stripped off his clothes and swam.

When he came out he felt younger, and came plodding up from the pool naked, carrying his clothes. In his path an old woman sat outside her wurley, gazing at nothing.

'I am one of you,' he said. '*Ngaia bendjin.*'

But she understood neither language, and did not look at him.

'I am your friend,' he said.

She reached out to touch her dog, which was growling, but did not move her head.

'Ah, you thing,' he said resentfully, 'you thing of dirt and wrinkles and pubic hair.'

He realized then that she was blind, and was filled with penitence, and went back to his camp under the rock where the foodbag was, and with his knife hacked open one of the precious tins. And he took it back to her and pushed pieces into her loose mouth. At first she struggled weakly to keep him away and turned her head from him, though she still kept her dog in order with one skinny hand. But then she tasted meat, and swallowed it, and turned to him with a grin that disclosed her great gums and the worn-down remnants of teeth just showing through them. He fed her until she was satisfied, and then she reached out and touched his shoulder with her hand, and leaned over and rested her forehead there. In that way they sat for what seemed a long time in that timeless place, naked brown woman by naked white man, and he stroked the loose skin of her back with tenderness, wanting to laugh, wanting to weep.

A man came out of the hotel and sat down with Dixon on a step. The street was dark and, except for the voices in the bar, silent. After a moment the man pulled out a mouth organ and played a sad, reedy tune.

'You work around here?' Dixon asked, when he had finished.

'Nah, not me. Queenslander.'

'Bit out of your way, aren't you?'

'I been working all up the coast here. Work the wharves a bit, get a bit of cash, and come on to the next place.'

'Like it?'

'What, the West? Jeez, I don't know how to answer you, mate.'

'Don't like it, by the sound.'

'I don't know. When you go to school you learn about these towns and you think they're real towns, like the ones we got over there. But when you come over and look at 'em — Christ, these aren't towns.'

'Give 'em a chance to grow. It's a big state.'

'I tell you what, mate, there's not a town north of Geraldton we'd call a town.'

'Looks like you'll be leaving pretty soon,' Dixon said.

'You bet your life. Darwin for me, then Isa, then Cairns. What's your lurk, mate?'

'Me? Stockman on a mission.'

'Mission? Christ. Any money in it?'

'No.'

'The wharves are good. I can pick up sixty quid, maybe, in a few days.'

'I make that in a year,' Dixon confessed, in a low voice.

'You're mad,' the man said, shocked.

'Maybe. I like it, that's all.'

'Tell you what, mate, you want someone to look after you. Come along with me for a while, pick up a bit of dough. Get a look at Australia.'

'I wouldn't mind,' Dixon said. 'I've got a job, that's all.'

'Chuck it in.'

'I can't,' Dixon said. 'No good talking about it. Give us a tune on that gadget of yours.'

The man shrugged and put the mouth organ to his lips, breaking into a cowboy melody. Nothing sounds sadder than one of those, Dixon thought, and nostalgia washed through him, the memory of nights around fires with the mouth organ for a background, and men holding forth strongly on their particular subjects, and himself no stranger.

But across the road, in the deep shadow of a store veranda, the black men were watching, waiting for the tide and for him. And he knew that he had made their country his, and their future his, and that many times in his first life he had been as lonely and as foreign as the mouth organ now made him feel. So he filled his mind with the rocky country up the river, and the thin music had no power over him.

Fires starred the darkness of the camp. Under his rock, behind his own fire, Heriot threw aside the remains of the piece of kangaroo Justin had brought him and sighed.

'That was good, eh?' Justin asked.

'Yes,' Heriot said. 'Yes.' He was weary to the point of collapse, and yet restless, unable to find any expression for his violent and disordered feelings.

From the darkness beyond the fires an old man began uncertainly to sing. A few more voices took him up, a sound weak and yet wild threaded through the valley. And Heriot, to a corroboree tune of tearing sadness, sang over them.

> 'This ae night, this ae night,
>   Every night and all,
> Fire and fleet and candlelight,
>   And Christ receive thy soul.'

'Don't, old man,' Justin whispered, shaken inwardly by the desolation of Heriot's voice.

> 'When thou from hence away art past,
>   Every night and all,
> To Whinny-muir thou com'st at last,
>   And Christ receive thy soul.'

'You go sleep now,' Justin pleaded. The valley was silent again, the invisible dark singers quelled. But there was no stopping the terrible voice of the naked white man.

> 'If ever thou gavest hosen and shoon,
>   Every night and all,
> Sit thee down and put them on:
>   And Christ receive thy soul.'

'Don't do that, old man.'

'I've given hosen and shoon.' Heriot said. 'Haven't I? And meat and drink. And a wife. And many years of my life.'

'You done that, old man.'

'I will pass,' Heriot muttered. 'Yes, I'll pass.' He went to sleep just as he lay. It was like the dying away of flame around a log.

Heriot dreamed, under his dark rock, of a surge of light pursuing him over the plains, crests and combers of flowing light reaching for him as he fled, in astonishment and terror, over the bare earth.

Oh God, cried Heriot, running for the hills, Oh God, preserve me.

A cliff rose out of the ground in front of him, he fell against it, seizing it with his hands. My hands, cried Heriot, looking at them. My quick, malicious hands. He would have stayed to stare at them, so intricately boned and veined, so subtly meshed; but the tide was coming and there was no time to stand, he clawed at the cliffs and climbed, his hands shaking, his feet slipping, beyond the boiling light.

Against the rock the waves broke in a brilliant surf, smashed into violet, indigo, green, yellow, orange, and red. All pure light, flowing and fractious, hungry for Heriot.

Give me strength, he cried, give me strength against the ravenous light. I am old and weak, too weak to bear annihilation. But his strength was gone and there could be no more climbing, he could only cling and pray as the breakers rose towards his feet.

The sun was blinded with the spray of them, time died, there was nothing but the light and the agony of waiting.

Now I become nothing, whispered Heriot, now and forever, for ever and ever, I am no more. He closed his eyes, waiting, clinging to the rock. No more, no more.

Then the intolerable sweetness washed over him. His hands slackened as he cried out, in astonishment and joy.

I am all light, cried Heriot, I am torn, I am torn apart, all light, all glorious light.

All elements and colours in him were resolved, each to return to its source below the enormous swell. And under the surf and into annihilation sank the last of Heriot's wild white hair.

Below the dark rock the sleeping Heriot waited for the ebb. It was a dream, he remembered, half-awake; a tired dream. But when the tide goes back, will there be nothing left, nothing but the bare earth under the cliff?

The tide began slowly to turn. But because of his dread Heriot could not wait for the uncovering of the ground, he began to shout: 'No! No!' and woke, shouting 'No!' under the black rock.

'Old man,' whispered Justin in the darkness, his voice strained with fear of the spirit that cried out in Heriot's body, 'what you got?'

'Nothing,' said Heriot. He put his hands across his eyes and sobbed like a child. 'Nothing. Nothing.'

7

When he woke again there was the rock hanging above his head, and he remembered all his journeying past cliffs rising out of their ruins, the huge size of the boulders that strewed the valleys, and the debris of vast and ancient landslides. Because of this his eyes fastened apprehensively on the cliff overhanging his sleeping-place; he saw the cracks in it, thought he saw them widen, thought he heard the grating of moving surfaces and sharp sounds of fission. He hauled himself upright on his aching bones and ran out into the camp area, shouting: 'Justin!'

Justin appeared, looking agile and young among the derelicts surrounding him, and very important with the rifle in his hand. 'What that, old man?'

'Let's go,' Heriot begged, 'before these cliffs fall. Let's go quickly, Justin.'

'Those cliff not going to fall, old man.'

'I want to go!'

'Hey, you look now,' Justin reasoned, 'these horse properly tired out now, you let them stay there where all that grass. Then we go tomorrow.'

Suddenly old and tremulous: 'I'm afraid,' Heriot said.

'Nothing going to hurt you, old man.'

'Justin,' Heriot pleaded, 'listen to me. Don't forget me now because I'm old and dying.'

'I listen to you all the time, old man. But I reckon better we stay here now and I go away getting tucker with my gun for this old people. You not dying, old man. You better go put your clothes on now, eh?' Embarrassment at the absurd appearance of the white man broke through the tolerant voice. 'It not right you walking round like that. You lie down sleeping all day, you feel good then.'

'I won't be one of these people,' Heriot protested hoarsely. 'I won't be so wretched. I'm not dead yet, I'm still strong, I can't — I can't — stop — now.' He turned away, shaking his head, and tears rolled down the cracks of his face. 'Ah, God —'

'You go and lie down now,' Justin said gently.

'Yes,' Heriot sobbed, 'yes.' He went back to his place under the rock and lay there and wept to himself at intervals through the whole day. At other times he slept, or lay stiff and still, his head swirling with meaningless and unconnected memories. Occasionally the silence of the valley would be broken by a shot in the hills above it, and once an aeroplane flew low over, heading west, and filled the whole place with its roar. Then there were a few shouts of alarm from the natives, but Heriot was neither startled nor curious. He registered only sounds outside and feelings inside himself. He was as simple as a child first come to light, and as bare.

The two stout women stopped by the hospital and leaned over the fence. On the veranda Rex sat propped up on a bed, reading a comic book. The women looked at him and at each other. Then one shouted: *'Gari!'*

He raised his head and considered them, unhappily.

'Gari! Na gari!' screamed the other woman.

'Bui!' he returned to them. *'Walea! Lewa!'* They were whores, they were bitches, in his opinion; he invited them to retire. *'Bui! Na gari, na!'*

When the women became abruptly silent he thought he had vanquished them, but in fact Helen had come out on the veranda and was watching the scene. 'What are they shouting?' she asked him. 'I keep hearing women screaming at you all morning. What does *gari* mean?'

He kept his eyes down and muttered after a moment: 'It mean: "You no-good." '

'That's unkind of them,' she said lightly.

'They say —' he began, and broke off.

'Well, what do they say?'

'They say Brother Heriot go away because I here. They reckon I make him sad and make him hate mission and he not coming back.'

'Oh,' she said softly. 'That's very hard.'

'And, sister, they reckon God hit me on the head that day because what I done to brother.'

'Oh,' she said.

'Might be that true, sister. Nobody know what hit me then.'

'No. Nobody knows.'

'Sister — i'n't somebody going looking for brother?'

'Yes, soon. The plane's looking for him now.'

'I go, sister?' He searched her eyes, pleadingly. 'I go?'

'No, Rex. You're not well enough.'

'I good now, sister. I got hard head on me, I not sick now.'

'You can't go,' she said, and turned her eyes away from the desperate resentment in his.

When she came into the room she was struck by the pallor of their faces, as she always was coming suddenly upon her fellow-Europeans. What a loathsome colour we are, she thought. All pink and disgusting. Why weren't we all made black?

She looked them over. Harris, wizened and balding, desperately thin, with his sudden, warm grin. Mrs Way, who might have been a grey-haired mistress in a girls' school, there was something so firm and widowlike about her. Way, rather shorter, rather heavier, with his sensible, dutiful face and tight mouth. Dixon, long, thin, and a little bent, with his sandy hair and narrow sunburned nose, his eyes that were abstracted or nervous. And the darker, finer, more compact Gunn, uneasy in his movements but stubborn in his expressions, eternally watchful.

'Well,' Way said, 'as we're all here, let's begin. I haven't much to say, I thought this would be more an opportunity for you to advise me. You all know the situation. Mr Heriot and Justin have gone, and we have to assume they went west through the hills; it's the most likely way. There aren't any tracks and we don't even know exactly when they left; only that it was on the day of the wind. The search plane went over this morning and may go again tomorrow. And the police have told me to send out a land party. That's the lot.'

'Who takes the land party?' Gunn asked.

'Looks like me,' said Dixon. 'Who else would it be?'

'Me.'

'Cut it out, Bob. We talked this over before.'

Harris said: 'We haven't heard. Talk it over again.'

Way tapped the table thoughtfully with a pencil. 'Since we had this out two weeks ago,' he said, 'I've been wondering more and more about it. I think I'm coming round to your point of view, Bob. Fact is that with things as they are I don't think I could carry on without Terry.'

'I'm afraid I've influenced him,' Mrs Way said. 'But you know, don't you, that I'm quite capable of coping with the school? I had two years with a small church school in India before we came to this country. So there's really no reason why Bob shouldn't go, if he'll trust me with his children.'

'But Bob's no bushman,' Dixon pointed out. 'What if you have to send me out to find him?'

'You're going too far,' Gunn said. 'Cut out these underhand gibes.'

Harris said: 'He doesn't need to be a bushman. All he needs to do is take Naldia with him and he'd be safe to go to Melbourne.'

'Who's Naldia?' Dixon asked.

'He's a bloke about fifty, one of the first children we ever took in here. But he went bush again when he was older. He knows that country better than anyone else his age. Talks a bit of English as well. You couldn't go wrong with him. He's up at the camp now.'

Gunn was beaming. 'Well,' said Dixon, 'that was short and sweet. Good luck, Bob.'

'Thanks.'

'Who're you taking with you?'

'Well, Naldia. I don't know about the rest. Paul might be a good man.'

'Take Stephen. He's busting to go. Seems to think it's partly his fault Heriot went off.'

'Rex thinks the same,' Helen said. 'Funny, isn't it? I think it's the first time they've seen a white man in bad trouble and they're all rallying round like anything.'

'I can't take Rex,' Gunn said, 'but Stephen's okay. We could go in the morning, if Harry'll fix us up with stores and Terry'll work out about the horses.'

Harris and Dixon murmured assurances, and a silence fell on the Ways' bare little living-room, to be broken at last by the hostess. 'Well,' she said, with pleasure, 'everything seems to have worked out very comfortably. And I must say I'm looking forward to having the school for a little while. I've often envied you, Bob, such dear children you have. Shall we have supper now?'

'I think we may,' Way said. 'Nobody wants to say anything else?'

'Yes,' Harris said, 'I want to wish you good luck with this super-intendent job. I've seen them come and go and I can pick a good one.'

'Second that,' Dixon said, and the others murmured.

'Well, I wasn't fishing for it,' Way said, with embarrassment, 'but thank you very much. It's only temporary, of course.'

'Heriot was only temporary,' Harris said. 'He had the job ten years.'

'Speech,' requested Gunn.

'I'm not used to making speeches —'

'Sermon, then.'

'Well, you know, I pledge myself to do the usual things as far as I possibly can. And I hope that in my time and in my successor's time we'll see some development in — well, in the relations between ourselves and the people. I hope we'll come closer and have the time and the staff eventually to make ourselves understood to them, teach them something of their own position in society, and their obligations, and their future. We're coming to a very bad time in the history of their development, and if we don't succeed in making contact with them and giving them some — orientation, the results could be unhappy for everyone. But with faith in them I think we'll come through. I ought to say that these ideas are as much Heriot's as mine, and when he spoke to me he was more or less handing over the problem to us. So if we succeed, we can feel that we're carrying out the plans that he hadn't the — opportunity of putting into action. That's really all I have to say.'

Now we feel happy, Helen thought, watching the faces. And hopeful. We know what we're doing. Is this very unkind of us, to feel so — relieved, now that Mr Heriot has gone?

Dixon grinned at her. Why is he watching me? she thought. And why have I been watching him, all through Father's speech?

82

There was Rex, lying awake on a dark veranda, crying in his mind: 'Ah, brother, where you now, eh? Where you now?'

And there was Heriot, asleep below his rock. 'Oh no, no, I couldn't take a life. An old, weak man like me? And such a strong young life, Rex's.'

And between them plain and hill, rock and grass and tree, mildly shining in the warm dark.

'I did wrong, the worst wrong a man can do. Who could have foreseen this, who could have thought this of *me?*'

'And might be I done wrong. Might be that girl dead 'cause of me. Ah, brother. Might be I ought to be dead.'

At Onmalmeri a dingo slunk out of shadow, hungry, scanning the valley with eye and ear and nostril for a hint of prey. And if it should kill, or, more conveniently, if it should come upon the putrid victim of a rival and steal it, what morality was infringed? How should that impede an easy sleep among the warm rocks?

'Ah, brother — They hating me now —'

'Oh, Rex, Rex, Rex. You will never go out of my mind.'

The sky was still grey when Heriot woke on the next morning, and he lay and watched the trees on the cliff top grow gradually sharper in outline against it, and the pool turn from gunmetal to deep green, and the sun stretch out its light along the valley to set the cliffs burning red and to waken glints of gold in the stems of canegrass. Nothing moved in the camp, and for once Justin had not wakened, but lay in a grey sheath of blanket at his side. Heriot reached out and touched him.

The figure shivered, waking. Then the head turned and the eyes were open, looking out from under the broad forehead. He had a beard now, with spikes of grey in it, and his hair was tangled. 'Good day, old man,' he said, yawning.

'Let's go soon. Now. Please.'

'Pretty soon we be going. You want tucker first.'

Heriot pushed away his blanket. 'Come with me,' he said, in his drained voice. His eyes were curiously empty, like those of the blind woman in the camp, and his mouth loose in the new beard. 'Come with me.'

Justin stood up, sighing resignedly. 'All right, old man. First I going to wash myself. You come down to pool.' He stepped out of the rock shelter and went down to the water's edge, Heriot slowly following like a stupid dog, and they stood in the pool and washed, while the birds woke in the leaves around them and the sun swelled red at the end of the valley.

They had come back and were dressed, and Justin was rolling the blankets, when he grew suddenly still and said in a voice of hopelessness: 'Old man, they pinch our tucker-bag.'

'Ah,' murmured Heriot.

'What we going to do now? We got no flour for damper and no tea and no sugar, old man. We going to starve.' His voice shook a little with self-pity, since damper and tea were the basis of his diet. 'Going to starve.'

The mad voice of Heriot broke into its wild keening.

> 'If ever thou gavest meat or drink,
>   Every night and all,
> The fire shall never make thee shrink;
>   And Christ receive thy soul.'

'Don't,' Justin shouted. He picked up the rifle and turned away, walking with angry determination into the camp. Then the bushes hid him.

Heriot sat down on the blankets and wailed to the echoing valley:

> 'If meat and drink thou ne'er gav'st nane,
>   Every night and all,
> The fire will burn thee to the bare bane;
>   And Christ receive thy soul.'

Across the valley came sounds of argument, Justin's voice raised in accusation, and Alunggu's angry and protesting. Silence followed, then a dog barked and a woman burst into a flood of invective or denial. Later Justin reappeared, a few tins piled in the crook of his arm and a scowl on his face, the outraged voices pursuing him like wasps.

'I get these tins,' he said curtly. 'That all they give me. Come on now. You carry them blanket, old man. I sick of carrying things all the time.'

They made their way back in silence along the valley, skirting the camp, Heriot stumbling a little on the rocks, for the rest of a day had worsened the stiffness in his body, though he was no longer as tired as he had been, filled instead with a restive and undirected energy. As he was dealing with the horses Justin let out a sudden shout and ran towards a cranny in the rock. When he returned he was grinning broadly, all his depression lost in the pride of a hunter. A long, yellow lizard with intricate brown marking hung limp from his raised hand, the red tongue curling out of the tapered snout.

'Beautiful, heraldic beast,' said Heriot, with deep sadness, reaching out to touch it.

They rode out of the valley and found a place where the horses could climb into the hills and pick their way clumsily and nervously over the rocks. Justin was now cheerful and talkative, with the sun lying clear but not yet burning on the surfaces of rocks and leaves, and the backward view of green plains and blue hills. 'They say there 'nother white man in this country,' he said. 'Might be we meet him.'

But Heriot's silence was unbreakable. They pushed on past the head of the valley and looked down on the bough-shelters of the natives, barely distinguishable from that height. And as they pulled up there to look for some sign of life, Justin said, weighing the rifle: 'Old man, this my gun, eh?'

They were horse by horse, and Heriot put out his hand and tore the rifle from the dark man, and threw it. It should have gone over the cliff, but it landed far short of the edge and lay on a clump of spinifex.

Justin jumped down to retrieve it, and stood on the ground with it in his hands, and stared widely at the wooden face of the white man.

'What for you do that, old man?'

'I want nothing,' Heriot said. 'When we all have nothing, then we can be equal.'

Weary after long travelling over the rocky tableland, Justin and Heriot came in mid-afternoon on a watercourse flowing shallowly over solid rock, and followed it, with the roar of water growing in their ears, until they reached a deep fold where the widened creek became a cataract and crashed over strata of rock to feed a larger stream below. The place was a horseshoe of stone, with crannied walls on either side, but the head of it was a vast, blackened staircase, each step flat and separate, over which the white water tore down to a boulder-dammed pool below.

Seeing this Heriot wakened a little from the dream which had enveloped him all day, and dismounted, and walked into the stream. Justin shouted: 'Old man, where you going?' but he did not answer. He took off his clothes and walked down the broad steps and lay under the white water, letting it beat and bludgeon his aching bones and drench his hair until in defence his strength came back and he grew hard under the assault. Reaching out, he could touch dry rock, and it was hot, but under the water he was cooled and renewed, and its sound and force shut out his aimless thoughts.

He did not hear Justin shout to him, and when at last he left the waterfall the man was gone. So he lay down on hot flat rock to dry and was half-asleep when Justin returned, wide-eyed with discovery.

'Old man,' he said urgently, 'there 'nother white man there.'

'He can't stop us,' said Heriot dreamily. 'I won't have it.'

'He camping down there in the creek. He got three horse, old man. We going down there, eh?'

'He can't stop me,' Heriot muttered defiantly. 'How did he find me? I wanted to be alone now. Tell him to go back.'

'You coming, old man?'

'No. Send him away.'

'I going,' Justin said, with a flash of irritation. 'You get you clothes on and come, too.' He went back to his horse and mounted, knowing that he had only to act decisively and Heriot would follow like a child. Presently the old man pulled on boots and trousers and came after him.

From the edge of the fold they could see three horses beside the creek, and as their own horses crashed and rattled down the slope a man got up from the shadow of a baobab and stood watching. A short man whose red hair showed clearly in the afternoon light.

He did not move, and they came up to him without a greeting, and he stared, a man of about forty, weatherbeaten, with a tangled red beard and shy at the eyes.

When their silence was becoming absurd: 'Didn't expect to meet anyone here,' he said diffidently to Heriot. 'Where you heading?'

Heriot said nothing. 'We going to coast,' Justin offered at last.

'Name's Rusty,' the man said, still to Heriot.

'His name Mr Heriot.'

'What's up with him? He dumb or something?'

'He sick in his head.'

'Too old for this country,' Rusty considered. 'You camping here?'

'You don't mind, eh?'

'No, go ahead. Better put your boss to bed, he looks buggered.'

'He all right,' Justin said, dismounting. 'Get down now, old man. We stay here now.'

With the stranger's eyes curiously and apprehensively on him Heriot slid off, still silent, his eyes, after a brief glance at the new face, returning to their state of far-sighted emptiness. Justin led him to the tree and sat him down there, and soon he turned on his side and went to sleep.

'Christ,' said the stranger, 'that's a queer boss you got, Jacky.'

He was quite a small man; wiry, hairy. And he was undisguisably furtive and uneasy in all his movements, even to the false casualness and muted tones of his voice, so that Justin was drawn into his mood and could think of no loyal denial to make. And they stood in silence, in a mutual retreat, and looked remotely down on the old man who lay fondling the earth in his wooden sleep.

The sun drifted behind rock hills, and the sky grew green. Later Justin lit a fire and cooked his goanna on it, filling the air with the stench of grilling fat.

'You ain't going to eat that,' Rusty said.

'He good, this.'

'You going to give it to the old bloke?'

'He like bush tucker,' Justin said defensively. 'You watch him.'

But when Heriot was wakened and a goanna leg thrust in his hand he could only take a few mouthfuls of it, then the fatty, faintly crablike taste disgusted him and he threw it away and lay down again and began softly to weep.

'Ah, cut it out,' said Rusty, shocked. 'Have a bit of tinned dog.' He pushed an open can into Heriot's hand. 'Jesus, don't bawl about it.'

The old man picked out pieces of meat with his fingers and ate slowly. Then he pushed the tin away.

'Where d'you come from?' Rusty asked.

Heriot stared through the fingered baobab leaves at the sky, which was deepening from green to aquamarine. The rush of the waterfall came clearly down from the hills. 'I come from Annalup,' he said, 'in the timber country.'

'Jesus,' said the man, startled.

The uncollected memories broke up in the old man's mind, became separate, fell into place. Old pictures returned to him, clearer than photographs, superimposed on the wild country of his wanderings. He saw an attainable peace at his fingers' end, reached for it, grief springing in him like a delicate green thing among the rocks.

'My father was a doctor. We had a house near the town. One of those grey, wooden houses. And some land. There was a creek and the arum lilies grew wild in it. It had high banks near the house and a log in the middle and you could sit there and no one knew you were there. They told me to sit and watch for the trout, but there weren't any trout. I was deceived,' said Heriot bitterly.

'Stiff,' said Rusty.

'You could go walking through the forests, through the karri. Huge trees, miles high, smooth, pale, no branches except at the top. When they cut them down, they tore the branches off other trees falling. When they hit the ground it jolted up through your shoes. It made a noise like a cannon.'

'Never seen that sort of country myself,' Rusty said.

'There were gullies full of ferns and blackberries.'

'I heard about blackberries,' the man said. 'Real weed, they say.'

'We'd go to the sea sometimes. It's green, then it's blue. In summer clouds pile up on the horizon and stay there. I said to my father: "What is that country?" and he said: "That is Antarctica." I was deceived.'

'They do that to kids.'

He saw rising out of the sea the white mountains, the crags, the fires.

> ' "Oh whaten a mountain is yon," she said,
>   "Sae dreary wi' frost and snae?"
> "O yon is the mountain o' Hell," he said,
>   "Where you and I will gae." '

'You know a bit of poetry,' Rusty said, with distrust.

'I was a clever man,' said Heriot strongly. 'I knew a good deal. But I lost it all, looking after my huts and houses. And now they've ruined me. Ah,' said Heriot, laughing, '*io fei giubetto a me delle mie case.*'

'What's the joke, mate?'

'My wit,' said Heriot weakly. 'My erudition. I knew French, too. *De nostre mal personne ne s'en rie, Mais priez Dieu que tous nous veuille absouldre.*'

'Go on.'

'I knew Spanish,' Heriot boasted, '*y se yo bien que muero por solo aquello que morir espero.*'

'You knew a lot,' the stranger granted.

'I knew German. *Owe war sint verswunden alliu miniu jar! Ist mir min leben getroumet, oder ist ez war?*'

Rusty shook his head, baffled.

'*Quod nunc es fueram, famosus in orbe, viator, et quod nunc ego sum, tuque futuris eris.* That's Latin,' explained Heriot, laughing feebly. 'I've forgotten my Greek. *Thalassa! Thalassa!* That will be useful soon.'

'What d'you do?' Rusty asked curiously. 'Schoolteacher?'

'Missionary.'

'Jesus, why?'

'I don't know. I had nothing to do and I was restless.'

'Funny sort of life for a man.'

'Once I was sick in hospital, one summer, and there was a sunset, one of those gaudy southern sunsets, and I looked out and saw a nun watching it, quite still, with a bedpan in her hand. I thought if I were a nun I'd feel like that, as if I'd earned the sunsets for myself.'

'You need a shave,' Rusty said, 'if you're going to be a nun.'

'Then I met a woman who had — that goodness. And I married her.'

'Happy ending, eh?'

'We weren't young. No. And she died after a few years. That was twenty-one years ago. But,' said Heriot with surprise, 'she was young, young to die.'

'You have stiff luck,' Rusty said.

'No,' Heriot protested. 'I didn't say that. I'm not sorry for myself, not now.' He fixed his awakened eyes on the man. 'You're wrong.'

'Okay, okay,' said the stranger irritably. 'I wasn't getting at you, mate.'

'No. No, I'm sorry,' said Heriot with remorse, 'forgive me.'

'She's right,' Rusty said. He had rolled a cigarette and lighted it from the fire, puffing smoke towards the old man, whose craving for tobacco woke at the smell. In the last days his miseries had lain on him like a heavy cloud, but now they began to separate out into fatigue and stiffness and homesickness, and hunger for such things as tea and tobacco. He held out his hand and asked humbly: 'Please, would you — would you give me some of your makings?'

'Go ahead,' Rusty invited, handing the tin. And as he watched the old man's fingers fumbling with the paper his thick mouth was touched with compassion. 'Tell us,' he said, 'where you're really going. Dinkum, now. What's the idea?'

But Heriot could not remember where he was going. He lit his cigarette and left it hanging from his mouth while he ran his fingers slowly through the tangle of white hair. It came back to him then, smokily.

'I'm exploring,' he said.

'What d'you want to explore this country for?'

'Not the country. No, not the country. I've found out — too much,' said Heriot sadly. 'Too much.'

'You got a real queer way of talking, mate.'

'Found weakness I didn't know of. And despair. And worse than that. But I'm beginning to come out of it, it's like waking, but I can't tell myself it was a dream. Oh, God, that's hard.'

'Listen,' said Rusty tentatively, 'what's the trouble? If I can give you a hand, you just got to ask.'

'What did Cain use against Abel?' Heriot demanded softly. 'Was it a stone?'

He began to notice for the first time the face of the man opposite, how the eyes gazed and shifted, how the mouth moved with a faint throb of the cheek below the beard.

'I wouldn't know, mate,' Rusty said warily. 'Don't go much on the Bible.'

'But the first murder was done with a stone. The first tool, the first weapon —'

'There was hands,' said Rusty quietly, and his own hands, bony and red-haired on the backs, tightened. 'Listen, what d'you want to talk about murder for?'

'It's a terrible thing. A terrible responsibility.'

'Cut it out,' Rusty said sharply.

Their eyes met, his red-brown eyes and Heriot's faded blue ones, in a strange and listening stillness. Then: 'They'll send a revenge party after me,' Heriot said. 'That is always done.'

'Shut up now!' Rusty shouted, breaking free of the old man's eyes and standing. 'What the hell are you talking about?'

'If I had strength,' Heriot said, 'I could go to those cliffs and break them. Then there'd be boulders, and I'd break them, and break them into smaller stones, and break them into pebbles.'

'Go ahead, if it'll shut your mouth while you're doing it.'

'Then I'd break the pebbles until there were molecules, and break the molecules into atoms.'

'Jesus, you're mad.'

'Then I'd break the atoms. They all have their moons, did you know, spinning round their own sun. I'd take that sun and break it into its protons and neutrons, and take the innermost of them and break it —'

'Well, go on, finish your bloody breaking.'

'And what if that should be God?'

The man came back and sat down hopelessly.

'The stone I killed him with,' said Heriot, 'was full of God.'

'Yes,' said the man in an empty voice.

'God was an accessory. He always is.'

'No,' said Rusty violently. 'God forgives you.'

89

'Your fingers forgive you, before you've used them. God is like that.'

'No. He pays us back for what we done.'

'We pay ourselves back. You know that. Because you know our crimes are like a stone, a stone again, thrown into a pool, and the ripples go on washing out until, a long time after we're gone, the whole world's rocked with them. Nothing's the same again after we've passed through.'

'I don't believe that,' Rusty said. 'No.'

'But you must. Why are you here?'

The man's hands were scaly on the backs, reddened with sun, never quite at rest. His eyes rose quickly to Heriot's, then, as quickly, hid under their sandy lashes.

'I come looking about the country. You never know, there might be something you could make a go of.'

'You must have money.'

'I've got a bit. What's it got to do with you?'

'I'm remembering,' said Heriot. 'Don't be afraid.'

'What are you getting at? What do you remember?'

'Something that happened a few years ago.'

'Well?'

'The Wet uncovered the skeleton of a white man buried in a creekbed.'

In the light of Justin's fire the man's eyes flicked up to meet Heriot's, and stayed there, burning a little with reflected light. Into them there came a curious expression, the expression perhaps of an escaped convict rescued by his own warders from country infested with tigersnakes and hostile blacks. Yet fear was dominant. He licked his lips, and swallowed, without intending it. 'You're mad,' he said flatly.

'No. Tell me.'

Behind their voices there was unvaryingly the roar of the waterfall, the quiet stirrings of horses. A faint wind coming up the gully touched the red beard.

'Listen,' Rusty said, 'listen. It wouldn't have been the money.'

'No, it wouldn't be. Not completely.'

'Supposing two blokes was camped out week after week in the Wet. They could drive each other crazy after a while.'

'Yes, they could.'

'Supposing one of them had a dog, say, and it kept coming into the tent.'

'And you said: "I'll shoot that dog if it comes again." And it came.'

'He went for me. What else could I do?'

'Your hands,' said Heriot, 'your wicked hands —'

'But I didn't mean to do it,' said Rusty harshly. 'I didn't mean it. Oh, Jesus, what do you want to know all this for?'

'And you buried him in the dry sand. But in another season the water came higher. He was there.'

'Three years, it was. Three years, waiting.'

'And you went on, working and wandering, as if nothing had happened.'

'But I kept wanting to go bush.'

'Why?'

'I don't know,' Rusty said vacantly. 'Don't know.'

'What do you do, out here, all alone? What do you think about?'

'I don't do nothing. I don't think, I just — I just wait for something to happen to me.'

'What?'

'I don't know. I just wait.'

'And nothing happens?'

'No, nothing.'

Heriot leaned back in the shadow. 'Nothing ever happens,' he said.

And truly nothing happened, though their strange, watchful understanding seemed to expect it. Only a sigh came from Justin in his sleep and a pebble rattled from the hoof of a horse.

'You ought,' said the man with the nervous hands, 'you ought to be scared of me. Yeah. You ought to be careful.'

Heriot put his hand over the clenched red one. 'You're not scared of me,' he said. 'No. We're all lost here.'

8

'What are you looking at, Paul?' Gunn asked.

The long-legged man shaded his eyes against the morning sun. 'Someone come up, brother,' he said, pointing back. 'Blackfellow, riding.'

After a moment Gunn picked out, among the low trees, the figure of the horseman. 'That's an old man, isn't it?' he said. 'He's got his hair tied up in a rag, like Naldia's.'

'Old man got no horse, brother.'

'Well, keep watching him,' Gunn said, and in a little time, while the rider was still to Gunn a shape of indistinguishable age, Paul murmured, with a painstaking concealment of surprise: 'That Rex, brother.'

'What?'

'It Rex, all right. I know him.'

'Well,' Gunn said quietly. 'Well.' And waited for Rex with a scowl growing on his face.

Rex also, when he came up, was frowning, uncertainly, and could not face Gunn and his disciplined anger. There was sweat on his face, below the bandage, and stubborn determination in his thick mouth.

'Well,' Gunn said again. 'You followed us.'

'Yes, brother.'

'Didn't bother to say good-bye to Sister Bond, I suppose?'

'He don't know, brother.'

'And where do you think you're going?'

'I — I want to go with you, brother. I want to help you looking for Brother Heriot.'

'You clot,' Gunn said viciously. 'You idiot. Do you think it's going to help us to have you tagging along, likely to get a haemorrhage at any minute?'

'I better now,' Rex protested. 'Sister Bond, he say that himself.'

'Did she say you could go riding round? In this country?'

Rex said defiantly: 'I want to go with you. You can't send me back now, brother.'

That was true, and Gunn's face admitted it. Ahead of them lay the untracked country, hiding somewhere among its blue bluffs and green pools two solitary men, and already it had been openly confessed that hope of finding them was on the ebb. And what is it to me, asked Gunn of himself, what is it to me if he chooses to put himself in danger? The old man's done more to earn his life.

'Well, you've messed us up properly. Hope you realize that.'

'I know. I sorry, brother.'

'Doesn't matter,' Gunn said sourly. 'Doesn't matter at all.' He turned away and left Rex to the curious attentions of Stephen.

'You ain't going,' Rusty said. 'Now?'

'It's a long way,' Heriot said. 'I don't even know how far.'

The red man looked up at him with the eyes of a lonely dog. 'Thought you was going to stay with me. After all we talked about —'

'No,' said Heriot remotely. 'That wouldn't be possible.'

'All I told you —'

'I know. I know it wasn't easy.'

'You listened to me. You knew what I was talking about.'

'Yes, I understood you.'

'Listen,' Rusty said, pleading with him, 'listen, I told you things no other bloke in the world knows. I felt good after that, I thought you was going to stick with me and — teach me things, about — God and all that. But you ain't the same bloke as what you was last night. Jesus,' said Rusty, 'you ask me what I feel like, and when I tell you, you don't care no more. What sort of a snooping bastard are you?'

'There's nothing I can do,' said Heriot, 'no way I can help you. All we could do for one another we did.'

'How's that?'

'We showed each other we weren't alone.'

'Just so we could be alone again?'

'I must go on. There might be — something, ahead of me.'

'I'll go with you,' Rusty offered. 'I got nowhere to go. Yeah, I'll come.'

'No one can,' said Heriot.

'What about the black? You're taking him, ain't you?'

'He'll come back,' Heriot said, 'in time.'

The other man sat down dejectedly on a rock and bit his thumbnail. 'Well, I can't stop you,' he said. 'This is mad. Every bloody thing's mad. I don't know.'

'It has happened before,' said Heriot, 'often, in this country. Hundreds of . . . outlaws, like you and me, in lost man's country.'

Rusty's forehead wrinkled under the red forelock. 'What are you running away from? What was it you done?'

'I wanted to kill someone,' Heriot said quietly. He stood woodenly by the rock with his stiff hands hanging down, and the wind moved in his white hair, and his eyes were empty as the sky. 'That was my — that brought me here.'

The other's eyes moved up his face, puzzled, looking for deceptions. 'Wanted to? Didn't you do it?'

'But that isn't important,' said Heriot, with faint surprise. 'It makes no difference at all.'

'Except to the bloke.'

Then new thoughts moved behind Heriot's eyes like yachts on an empty sea, and for the first time he remembered Rex alive, and what it must have been to be Rex, to take pleasure in clothes and women, to be sullen and rebellious and know the causes, to suffer injustices and to invent injustices in order to resent them. He thought of Rex dancing by canegrass fire and delighting in the rhythms of his body, or subsiding into sleep under shade at midday, or swimming, or hunting, or sitting round a fire at night talking or singing to a guitar. Rex's life presented itself whole to him, the struggle against sordor, and then the defiant return to sordor, and the bitter pride underlying it; the old tribal grievances, real or inflated by legend; the fights and the humiliations, the quick gestures of generosity and the twists of cruelty; all the ugly, aspiring, perverse passions of a living man.

'Now I know,' he said from a great distance, 'I know why I'm going on.'

'Why's that?' asked the man, soft as canegrass in the wind.

'Because all this time I've been deceiving myself. Telling myself I was old and weak, and I'm not. Telling myself I wanted to die, but I don't, no, and I never will. All this has been self-pity, nothing else.'

He scrubbed his forehead with a brown fist. 'Now I remember — the things I used to know.'

'What?' asked the man, still intently watching. 'What did you know?'

'About crimes. About being born out of crimes. It was because of murders that I was ever born in this country. It was because of murders my first amoebic ancestor ever survived to be my ancestor. Every day in my life murders are done to protect me. People are taught how to murder because of me. Oh, God,' said Heriot savagely, 'if there was a God this filthy Australian, British, human blood would have been dried up in me with a thunderbolt when I was born.'

'You can't help being born, mate.'

'I'm glad to have been born now. This is a good time for it, with the world dying. The crimes have mounted up now, we can sit and enjoy the stink of our own rot.'

He turned away, his eyes full of the farther hills. 'I know life comes out of crimes,' he said, 'and we go on from one crime to another, and only death ever quite stops us. I could go back and they could hang me, and that would put an end to it. But all my life I've stopped off, here and there, to try to do some good on my way. I've tried to atone for being a man, and now it's a habit. So I have to go on, this way, where there might be

94

something to do besides die. The other way there's nothing, only dying. But on this way I've already given — not much, but a little, a little food, a little cold comfort. There may still be things to do, and things to find.'

The other man looked down at the rocks between his feet. 'Well,' he said, 'it's been nice seeing you.' His voice was lonely.

'Yes,' said Heriot. 'This has been — this has been an oasis to me. But we say good-bye to everything.' He held out his hand and the other man took it, glancing up moodily from his rock.

On the wire screen, bellies to the interior light, little pale geckos and green frogs clung and slowly breathed, twitching occasionally to engulf a mosquito.

'Ah,' said Dido, mountainously stirring, 'he was a good man. Too good for natives. Maybe he was hard, but they got to be hard some time.'

Helen said: 'But was he so hard? I think he was only — well, just a bit bitter.'

'In the old days they was hard. They had to be like that, not soft like now.'

'Do you think we're too soft?'

Dido looked down at her locked fingers, distress spreading over the moon face. 'There lot of no-good people here now. Lot of men, just lazy, gambling all the time, bad husbands. Lot of no-good women, too, not looking after their babies right.'

'There are no-good people everywhere, Dido.'

'He was example,' Dido said passionately, 'example to us all.'

'I know. If you mean hardness in the way he had it, towards himself, I can see you're right. We haven't that.'

'Because you young, sister.'

'I'm not so terribly young, you know. You think I'm younger than I am because I'm not married and haven't any children.'

'When you married, sister, you be good example to all the women. I know that, sister.'

Helen smiled faintly. 'Thank you, Dido.'

'But we never see him again,' said Dido sadly. 'Never.'

'But can't we ever replace him? We'll be softer, and our example will be softer, too, but isn't it time for that now? We don't want to be your bosses, we only want to show you things.'

'Too many no-goods,' Dido said. 'You got to be hard some time.'

'But they aren't all no-goods. What about Michael, and Gregory, and Paul, and Justin, and Ella, and you, Dido? You're the ones who know what you live for and have something to be proud of. Michael's a good man because he knows he's the best mechanic of all you people. And Gregory's good because he's the best gardener, and Paul's the best stockman, and Justin's the sacristan of the church, and Ella loves Justin and her children, and you love your orphans and have all the

95

responsibilities of a white woman. And in time I think everyone will be good at something — why not? And who'll need to be hard then?'

Dido shook her head slowly. 'That not going to be easy, sister.'

'I know,' said Helen, looking at the peering creatures on the screen. 'It's certainly not going to be easy for us, the white people. Living in a goldfish bowl is the last thing we'd do for fun. And as long as we live here we can never be ourselves, unless our selves — break out, like Mr Heriot's. But that won't happen. No,' she said, with profound resignation, 'that can't happen, Dido.'

The sun stings, thought Heriot. Yes, it stings. He remembered from long ago a banana plantation he had seen, the great leaves closing out the light, a trickle of water in the sweet earth between the stems. That would be a place for an old man to work, a cool place, with the fruit hanging in green chandeliers over his head, fresh and fragrant. He would never go out in the sun if he had such a place to hide in.

But he had nowhere to hide, there was no shelter in the country of rocks, and no movement, nothing to rest or entertain the eye. He thought of cattle breaking away across a creek, the splashing and the bellows, the shouts of the bright-shirted men pursuing on shining horses. There was no action here.

And it was silent, too, so silent that again and again he had this urge to sing and drown out the silence, although the sound of his voice was hardly less disturbing. If there were music, he thought; but why should I care for music, how many years is it since I have heard music? Only the people's voices shouting hymns or cowboy songs, and sometimes, in the firelight and the moonlight, the didgeridoo. But that was uplifting, there was a ranting throb to it, it compelled you to sing with it in its own style. But he would not hear that again.

He remembered Stephen dancing in front of the fire, and Rex, too, supple and quick. Strange how Rex's face haunted him now, how it hurt him to remember, almost as much as the face of the dead girl, Esther, whom Rex had taken from him. There were expressions of Rex's, quick movements of the head, twists of the mouth, that touched him now very deeply. He remembered the last afternoon when he had found Rex alone at the deserted building, and even then had thought him pathetic, even then had wished to help him.

'I didn't hate Rex,' he said. 'Remember that.'

'I remember,' said Justin.

He, too, was reaching back in his mind, thinking of Ella, his wife, and the quiet affectionate children. I go back, he thought, soon, soon. But he could not bring himself to speak of it to the old man, who was now changed again, had regained strength, and yet still seemed so much in need of help, so far from knowing the ends of his journey.

'What can we do about Stephen?' Heriot said. 'He must be helped.'

'Might be I help him, brother.'

'You could, Justin. Perhaps you're the only one who could. I don't know anyone who's raised better children than you and Ella.'

'He Ella's cousin, you know. Maybe I talk to him when we get back. Maybe.'

'You're a good man,' said Heriot. 'You'll know what to do, when you get back.'

'I try, brother,' Justin said modestly.

'And help Way and the other white people, too. They'll need your help.'

'Might be.'

'I'm afraid I've never made the best use of you. But I do know your value, I do know that.'

Justin scowled. 'Brother —'

'Yes?'

'I don't want to talk so much. I too hungry for talking.'

'I'm sorry,' said Heriot humbly.

'White man always talking and never listening.'

'That's true,' Heriot admitted. 'Very true.'

'Whatever you say to white man, he always got something else to say. Always got to be the last one.'

'We call it conversation,' Heriot said, and bit his lip as soon as the words were out.

So they rode in silence over miles of the broken hills, and came in the afternoon to a place where the land dropped sharply down to a pocket of plain dotted with white gums, and a broad river flowing beside a cliff.

'Beautiful,' whispered Heriot. 'How cool —' The horses bashed and strained down the hillside, and stopped, sweating and trembling, in the shade, knee-deep in grass. The water ran with a rippling monotone over a bed of rock. 'How cool, how calm.'

'We camp here?' asked Justin.

But Heriot, having arrived at such comfort, felt half-afraid to accept it, to indulge his tired body. 'It's early to camp,' he said. 'We'll have to cross the river some time. Why not now?'

Justin shrugged. 'If you want that.'

'Why put it off?' asked Heriot, urging his horse forward. 'We postpone too much. I haven't much time.'

'The horses tired. You don't want to kill them, brother.'

'I'm tired, too,' said Heriot.

'All right,' Justin said resignedly. 'We cross over.'

They moved to the river's edge and dismounted to drink. The water was full of islands of pandanus, scraping a little in a light breeze, and below the cliff it was dark, bottomless. 'I could catch little croc there,' Justin said.

'When we cross,' Heriot said impatiently. He was in the saddle again,

97

scanning the river at the end of the cliff where the water was shallower. 'There's the place.'

Under the horses' hoofs the river-rock was slimy and treacherous, they slipped like skaters, and Heriot sat tense in the saddle, willing Albert Creek to stay upright. And yet he had no nervousness, no doubt that the horse would come safely over. He went ahead of Justin to the middle of the stream, where it squeezed itself out in strong currents from between the palm islands. And there the rock went down a sudden step, the horse slithered, wildly threw up his head, and sank.

The old man, floundering in the water, his hair in his eyes, struck out against the current towards Justin. The sharp edge of the rock step struck him on the shin, tearing deep through his flesh. But he scarcely noticed it. For he was terribly afraid of death.

Justin was edging his horse towards him, uncertain whether to abandon it for Heriot. 'Old man!' he shouted harshly. 'This way, this way!' And the old man rose trembling and dripping from the water, reached out for him and fell against the horse, gripping Justin's leg. 'Dear God,' he whispered, panting against the warm wet side of the beast.

'Ah,' said Justin, sighing, 'you safe now.'

Heriot looked along the river. But of his quiet and weary horse, his first companion on his journey, there was no trace. 'He gone floating down to deep water,' Justin said. 'He gone now.'

'He was a good horse,' Heriot said, eager to speak well of the dead. 'Poor Albert Creek.' He shook his head.

'No good being sad,' Justin said. 'You keep holding me and we get across this time.'

Sliding and stumbling on the precarious riverbed, they did at last reach the farther bank, beyond the cliff, and came to a stop behind a thicket of pandanus.

Justin was seized with laughter, looking down at the old man with his bedraggled hair and dripping clothes. 'You look real funny,' he said. 'Real funny,' his shoulders shaking.

'This is a great misfortune,' Heriot said gravely. 'I can't see anything funny in it.' He quivered, and dissolved into weak laughter. 'Nothing funny at all. Stop that, Justin.'

'You stop,' Justin protested. 'You making me laugh.'

'How stupid,' said Heriot, rocking helplessly. 'Idiotic. Quiet, man.' Tears came into his eyes and his upper teeth fell out. He picked them up and with dignity replaced them, while Justin heaved hysterically on the back of the startled horse.

'For God's sake,' said Heriot, sitting on the ground, 'stop this cackling and think of the future.'

'You mean supper, brother?'

'Well, that would be a start.'

'I go looking for little croc, eh?'

'I could eat a horse,' said Heriot.

'All right, I get that horse for you.'

'No. I fancy a crocodile tail more.'

'*Gare*,' said Justin obligingly. He dismounted and unsaddled his own horse. 'Poor old horse, he real tired now. Going to be lonely now, got no brother any more. Look 'im, eh, he crying out of his eyes.'

'Yes,' said Heriot. 'He's all alone.'

'I go now, brother,' Justin said, his spear in his hand. 'I bring you tucker pretty quick. Real good tucker, just you wait,' he promised, disappearing among the pandanus.

'Yes,' said Heriot vaguely. He pulled up his trouser leg and looked at the cut on his shin. Clean, he thought; leave it. He pulled off his shirt and spread it in the sun. Soon be dry, soon be hot again.

All alone now. It's a very desolate sound, pandanus leaves. Funny to have been laughing like that, it was almost like being with Esther, she made one laugh. Clever, satirical girl. She would leave me helpless, imitating Dido in a quarrel. Stephen's not like her.

He had said to Justin, not seriously, to think of the future. But himself he was absorbed in the past, remembering Esther, with her slim grace, her natural charity. It had been tempting providence, surely, to have been so proud of her; but it was I who should have suffered for my pride, not Esther, not my daughter.

His mind grew vacant, soothed by the hush of water, the rattling leaves. The sky took on the faint green tinge of sunset. Later Justin returned, proudly carrying the young freshwater crocodile he had ambushed below the cliff.

'Handsome beast,' Heriot said. 'Clear-cut delicate features. Had a happy life until we came.'

'There plenty eggs,' Justin said. 'You want one?'

'No,' said Heriot. He lay back and closed his eyes. The reptile cooked on the fire. The old man's hunger died, and he fell asleep.

9

The river bent, disclosing a stretch of plain running to farther hills, an ocean of knee-high grass sweetly green in the early light. From the horse's hoofs a bundle of quail rose and whirred away. And the old man drew rein and slipped from the saddle, his weariness reaching out towards all that was green and soft, and said: 'You ride, Justin, I want to walk now.' He stretched in the sun and smiled with his ill-fitting teeth, while the white hair flapped on his forehead. 'This is a glorious day,' he said, 'isn't this a glorious day?'

'It real good, brother,' the dark man said, and he, too, was happy, with the smell of warm and deep grass rising to him and a clear pool with a few lilies ahead.

'Look at the birds,' Heriot said. 'Brolgas.' He pointed to where, not far from them, a great flock of grey-blue birds was gathered, and three or four of them were dancing, measured and graceful, with a flowing interplay of wide wing and thin leg. 'They're happy,' said Heriot.

'They always happy, those brolga.'

'Why aren't we like them, Justin? It shouldn't take so much to content us.'

'I happy, brother,' Justin said, with a wide grin. 'I just a bit hungry, that all.'

'Everything's hungry,' said Heriot sadly. 'But look at those ducks, they're happy, just pushing among the lilies, getting what they can. So pretty, and so stupid. Wouldn't you like to be a duck, Justin?'

'I like to eat a duck, brother.'

'No, don't kill anything. Not this morning. Just for one morning let's not prey on anything.'

'People got to eat, brother.'

'Why?' asked Heriot, glancing up at him dejectedly. 'God, what malice must have gone into creating a world where people have to eat. I renounce it.'

They came to the edge of the pool, and with a great splash and a clap of wings the ducks fled from their coming, and circled above and above the disturbed waterhole, brown ducks and black ones, and the small delicate teal, in a high outcry of whistling. By the water, between low cadjiputs, Heriot paused, watching the flitting of a dragonfly with a gleaming crimson body, and became suddenly aware of four pelicans, undisturbed

100

on the far bank, regarding him sedately with their absurd eyes of black-and-yellow felt. 'Ah, you beauties,' he said, 'you bench of uncorruptible judges.'

A shot cracked the air. The pelicans flapped heavily and flew off.

Turning, slow with shock: 'You didn't,' Heriot said desolately, 'you didn't shoot at a pelican. Justin —'

'It were a geese, brother,' said the brown man, already at the pool's edge and tearing off his clothes. 'I got him. You wait, good tucker.' He burst into laughter, wading and swimming across the pool, and in the water by the other bank picked up the limp black-and-white body and held it up to be admired. 'Fat one, brother, young fella.'

But Heriot's eyes had moved to the lone black jabiru which had risen from somewhere when the man entered the water and was now gliding, long and calm, across the sky. When the goose plumped at his feet he started, and saw with ineffable sadness the claws of the brilliant yellow legs bent like dying hands, the perfect and ingenious groovings on the edges of the beak. 'That was pretty,' he said, 'and happy.'

Justin fondled it, tender and proud. 'Good little geese,' he said with affection. 'You was pretty fella, eh? Poor old geese.'

'You love the things you kill,' Heriot said, 'but you never regret killing them. I've noticed that always about you people, how you love your prey. There's some wisdom there.'

'They pretty,' Justin said.

'Let's go and look at them,' Heriot said, 'all these pretty things. I want to watch them all day. They're very dear.' He walked on down the pool, followed presently by Justin, who shouted from the saddle: '*Dor!*'

'What?' asked Heriot vaguely.

'You look in water there. There, look.' And close beside him he saw the body of a python, great pale coils and small head floating among the lilies.

'Bin drown himself,' Justin said, laughing.

But to Heriot this death was too sad for comment, and he walked all day in a mist of love and grief, pausing to peer at a peering blanket lizard on a tree trunk, pausing to point out two grotesque, loose-bustled emus to Justin, who roared with laughter. '*Wieri!*' he said, with ridicule and tenderness, loving them for their absurdity. 'Like fat old woman, bum too big to carry.'

And in the late afternoon Justin called softly: '*Banar*, there look,' and slipped from the saddle with the rifle under his arm. And Heriot, straining his eyes, saw above the grass the long necks and flat heads of a pair of turkeys. 'Don't,' he said, but the dark man was already intent on them and only answered with a shot which sent one bird to the sky and the other leaping and flapping about the grass. He plunged after it and wrung its neck, and came back to show it proudly to Heriot. 'We have feed tonight, brother,' he promised.

'Yes,' said Heriot. 'Yes.' He reached out and touched the pale-brown feathers, felt their crêpey texture and smelt the bitter body. 'We're very dangerous to the world,' he said sadly.

Coming towards the foothills where they camped that night their ears were attacked by the harsh throb of a kookaburra, and the light flashed on the brilliant blue of its wings. Simultaneously a flock of ibis crossed the dim sky, sharply and perfectly angled as in a Chinese painting, and one of them was white, but was washed rose in the light of the fallen sun. 'My beauty,' whispered Heriot, 'my perfect one.'

That night, lying by the fire, his eyes and ears were strained to overhear and interpret every sound and movement of the earth, so that the brief appearance of flying-foxes in the firelight was as beautiful as the soaring of a flock of parrots at dawn, and the howling of dingoes, that once had tugged at his nerves, was no longer predatory but wistful, and moved pity in him, for he thought they lamented.

All the next day they climbed in the hills, but now there was no water, only the bare rock and the stunted trees, and all day, walking or riding, Heriot withered in the heat. After a time he could not find strength to talk, with his tongue dry and the breath short in the lungs, and Justin also was silent, perhaps afraid. In Heriot's mind rock and tree, to which with eye and flesh he clung, needing their solidity to convince him of his own, wavered and faded, and he saw his bleak room at the mission and everything that was in it. He read the labels on bottles. He saw the room in the Ways' house that had been their bedroom, his and Margaret's, and he saw her, with the sheet thrust back in a movement of fever from her frail body, and her hair across the pillow. No one but himself had ever noticed the few threads of grey.

'In these last years,' he had said, holding her hand, 'I've never felt there was any need to tell you — because I knew you'd know — that I love you, Margaret.' His voice was shaking then, and it never had before. 'My dear, my dear.'

But she had only moved her head on the pillow and he had not been able to tell whether she was impatient with him or whether she was simply past hearing.

And he had gone on in a rambling murmur, protesting his love, daring even to mention the child, consoling her as he had not once attempted before for the agony of her miscarriage and the rough ignorant hands of the black midwife and the kind, ignorant voices of the women year after year questioning her about her childlessness. But it was too late then to waken her to him, even with reminders of that ancient grief, and she wanted no sympathy or consolation, only relief from pain. So he had knelt by her and prayed, still holding her hand, but how could he pray with the pain twisting in her body, moving through her fingers and crying to him, how could he address God unless as an enemy?

And when she was dead he had rested his cheek for a moment against her hand, and gone out blindly into the sunlight where Mark and Emily were waiting, he carrying the child on his shoulder, she leaning against a tree with the curve of her pregnancy showing under the grimy dress. They had no word to say to him, but they could speak without speaking. And Mark had held out the child to him, and said: 'Stephen here, *abula*, look 'im, eh'; and he had taken Stephen, and when the terrible keening of the women began, the child's wails of alarm had drowned it, drowned everything but the will to give comfort.

All through that day he carried, as nagging as his thirst, the memory of Margaret and the futility of his love, and the memory of Stephen, and the dearer memory of Esther, waiting then in the dark womb of her mother to be his consolation and his despair.

At night they were still in the hills and still without water. And Justin, in the brief dusk, went prowling among rocks in search of game, and came back at last, reliable as ever but unsmiling, with a dead euro slung over his shoulder. 'You better drink that blood,' he said curtly.

Pity and love stirred in the old man for the delicate ears of the dead kangaroo, the deep soft eyes. He touched the fine fur, ran his fingers through it, and felt a tick under his hand. 'What is there that isn't preyed upon?' he said, all his sadness wakened to find such filth feeding on such beauty.

In the night they lay uneasily, sleepless, their fears colliding and rebounding in darkness.

'Are you asleep, Justin?'

'No, brother.'

'I think — tomorrow —'

'You go sleep now, brother.'

'Promise you'll leave me — take care of yourself —'

'Nothing going to happen to you —'

'Justin?'

'Yeah?'

'Promise me. Don't let me prey on you.'

'I sleepy now, brother.'

'Yes, but promise.'

'I promise. Brother —'

'Yes?'

'There only two more bullets left.'

'Keep them. For when you go back.'

'Yes. Yes. Go sleep now, please.'

In the morning they were driven by thirst and insects to rise and wander on before the sun was up. And at dawn they crossed a steep ridge, and below them was a river, and on the river a town.

'No,' said Heriot. 'This is not real.'

And yet it was solid, its handful of shacks flanking a dusty, grass-grown road, its roofs shining a little redly with rust in the sun. There were two larger houses and a building with wide verandas. 'That is the hotel,' said Heriot.

The river swept around it, between the hills and the short stretch of plain, and, shaded by baobabs, the piles of a small ruined landing-stage reached out of the brown water. Brown water. 'That river salt water,' Justin exclaimed.

'No,' said Heriot. 'It's not real.'

'Come down, brother, quick,' urged the dark man. He began picking his way down the rocky hill, leading the horse, impatient, driven on by thirst and a sudden rebellion against the futility of their wandering.

And the old man, stumbling after him, had the same consciousness of futility hardening in him. He was weak, and sick, and tired, and here was an end to the journey for which he had planned no end, here was an un-chosen goal. He said: 'Justin.'

'What, brother?'

'I'll finish here. I'll go into the hotel and say who I am. They'll know what to do with me.'

There was silence from Justin until they reached the plain. Then: 'You know best, brother,' he said diffidently.

'I do, Justin. This has been useless, all of it. I'll be peaceful now.'

They pushed on through the grass towards the road, and the grass was knee-high and drying, but in one patch it was tall and green. 'There water there,' Justin said, stepping towards it. But it was only a sort of crater that had held water for a time and lost it. 'No good,' he said, in the flat and stoical voice that had become habitual to him.

Heriot had reached the road and was walking down it, straighter now and stronger in his resolution. Here and there, withdrawn from the track, decrepit shanties stood deep in grass and silence. 'Native houses,' he said, 'and all asleep. Everyone sleeping,' a strange and gentle envy in his voice.

But he was intent on the larger building, and when he came to it, with Justin slowly following, he stopped still in the road and his hands began to tremble. Two of its veranda posts were broken, floor-boards were missing, the wooden steps lay in the grass. He turned suddenly to Justin for reassurance. 'Suppose nobody's at home?'

'You write them a letter then,' Justin suggested, weakly attempting his grin.

'Wait,' said Heriot, 'wait here.' He stepped up on to the veranda, and an ant-eaten board gave way, so that he stumbled, dragging back his foot, against the door, and it opened on a long room. Dust lay over the holed floor and on a couple of wooden benches and on a collapsed table. But beyond that there was nothing, only a little dust that danced, stirred by the door's opening, in sunlight falling obliquely through the steel-meshed window.

Until that moment it had hardly occurred to him, weary and sun-

104

drugged as he was, to wonder what this town might be and why it was there. But there was a familiarity about the scene that troubled him, and slowly, through his early morning torpor, memory returned. He said: 'But it's a dining-room —' And at the same time Justin called out: 'Brother! Brother, this not a town. This Gurandja, brother.'

Not a town, no, an abandoned mission. A ghost mission. Gurandja, fifteen years dead.

He turned and crossed the veranda, stepped down to the grass and came blindly back to Justin. 'Nothing,' he said. 'Nothing. Nothing.'

He had never looked so old, standing there in the road with his white hair falling down and the dust caked in the ruts of his face and on his stiff, white beard. His hands hung down crooked as driftwood against the torn trousers, and his eyes were equally still, empty and unblinking, though the light stung them like smoke. 'But this must be the end,' he said, in wonder. 'Must be.'

Justin's face above the black beard was a stoic mask. But beneath the jutting forehead his eyes, deeply glowing as always, deeply watchful, rested on the old man's with a helpless compassion, and a quiet despair. In the dead town they were still as the dead. Only the horse twitched and stamped a little with tired, restless life.

'Well,' said Heriot with his wooden lips, 'it may be all. Yes, it may. I'm very weary, Justin.'

'We go look for water, eh? There be water somewhere here, I reckon.'

'Water?' said Heriot. 'Yes. Yes, there'll be water.' He moved forward down the road, slow as a sleepwalker. 'We'll look.'

Justin, following, leading the horse, searched with his eyes the long grass, the abandoned houses, but saw no sign of water, only the brown salt river in the distance. Yet there was luxuriance all around, young baobabs springing up even out of the road, giant greentrees pushing against houses, and here and there a sprawling oleander in full bloom. And the largest of the houses, the mission house, was being slowly torn down by a vast bougainvillaea smothered in purple bracts. Beyond, over a house at the edge of the village, the blue air stirred, distorting the hills behind it, so that they seemed to shimmer through a column of clear water. The brown man's eyes widened.

'Brother,' he said, softly, it being now very important to him not to excite Heriot, 'brother, you look there.'

The old man followed the line of the dark finger, and found nothing. 'What?' he said. 'Look at what?'

'That smoke, brother.'

'Smoke?' said Heriot dully. 'I don't see it. Your eyes are tired.'

'You come with me,' Justin said, 'you come.' He turned off the road, the horse and Heriot behind him; and as they came towards the house the old man saw the smoke, and saw the green tangle of a vegetable garden around a fenced-off spring, and a mob of goats deep in grass farther away, and he sighed.

'Don't be sad,' Justin said. 'We all right now.'

There was a fence around the shanty, and they climbed over it, as there was no gate to be seen. 'Now,' said Justin, half-whispering, 'you go, brother. I reckon that white man there.' He hung back, waiting for the old man to approach.

Very slowly Heriot walked towards the hut. It was a one-roomed structure with a veranda shading the bare ground outside it, and had a blind look, with its closed shutters and door of warped packing-case boards. He reached out and knocked, hesitantly, with his blotched hand.

The door swung inward with a long, weary sigh. There was a goat standing there, watching him with long, yellow eyes and an expression of uncritical pleasure.

Crows were crying around the spring, but otherwise there was no sound, the world lay asleep in the still light and the goat stood as if carved out of some pale stone. Oh, God, thought Heriot, for a sound, someone chopping wood, a native singing. As if to answer him there was a sudden flap and crow of a cock somewhere near at hand. His nerves jumped.

'Nothing?' said Justin, coming behind him. His face was wet, he had been at the spring.

'No,' said Heriot. He burned in sudden anger, his dignity affronted. 'What trick is this? The goat didn't open the door. Not a goat. I am deceived,' he said bitterly, turning and looking through the light towards the spring, green with lank cabbages and pumpkin vines. He yearned for the cool smell of leaves, the cooler run of water over his face. 'Someone lives here,' he said, 'and doesn't want us. Well, I'll wash in his spring, let him come out then if he wants to stop me.'

'Piss in his spring,' said Justin. He was grinning. Then his eyes came back from the garden and rested on the door, and the grin dwindled. 'Brother,' he whispered tensely.

'What is it?' asked Heriot, the imagined water already on his face, his skin sucking it in, his body relaxing in almost forgotten comfort. 'What are you staring at?'

The goat stretched its throat and bleated.

'Someone eye watching us,' Justin whispered.

'What? Where?'

'In the door. There, look.'

Heriot, turning, followed the pointer of the brown finger and found the crack in the door; through which, as the sunblind lifted from his sight, an eye became visible.

'You come away,' Justin said. 'Quick. Might be he kill you, brother.'

'Hush,' said Heriot. He watched the eye with anger and dislike and said nothing. And the eye, faded blue and veined, was non-committal.

'Man,' said Heriot, 'if you are a man, come out. I've come a great many miles and this is discourteous.' He grinned with his crooked teeth. 'If you're mad, come out, we'll be mad together.'

Silence returned. The goat had retreated into the shack and was waiting, also motionless.

'I'll give you ten seconds,' said Heriot savagely, 'then I'll come and put my fist in your disgusting eye.'

Slowly, from behind the door, an old man appeared, shambling in bare feet, a length of rusty iron in his hand. He was the colour of dirt from the ragged bottoms of his trousers to the straggles of his hair. Above his dusty beard was a face marked like dry creek country, with deep and gritty lines. Only the pale eyes seemed made of living tissue.

'Good morning,' said Heriot.

'You'll black my eye, will you?' the old man said venomously. 'Call me mad? I could take the scalp off you.'

'Put down that weapon,' Heriot ordered.

'Fists'll do,' said the old man, dropping the iron. 'You try it, mate.' He spread his feet and raised two bony fists, the aggressive stance making more obvious the emaciation of his body and its tremulous weakness. Heriot, moving away without loss of dignity, said gravely: 'Please, be calm. Now that I see you *in toto*, I'm truly sorry.'

They looked at one another, then slid their eyes away. Through the blazing light the spring showed cool and green, so that to look at it was, for both of them, peaceful. The old man, backing a few steps to lean against the mud-wall of the shack, said with sudden friendliness: 'Ain't me that's mad. You're the one.'

Heriot bowed his head.

'What's your name?' the old man demanded.

'Heriot.'

'What Heriot?'

'Just Heriot.'

The old man grunted. At the side of the shack the rooster crowed and flapped again. What sleepier sound could there be, thought Heriot, in the hot sun, when you're tired to the point of dying? He came over to the old man and propped himself on the wall beside him. Justin was squatting ten yards away, watching them. 'Cheeky bastard,' muttered the old man, catching his eye.

Heriot yawned. As if by arrangement he and the old man let their backs slide down the wall until they were sitting on the ground.

'Have you lived here long,' Heriot asked, 'Mr —?'

'Sam,' said the old man.

'Sam,' said Heriot. Silence fell again.

After a long lapse Sam inquired drowsily: 'You wouldn't — no, you wouldn't have a smoke, would you?'

'No,' said Heriot with regret. 'I'm trying to give it up.'

'Haven't had one for two years.'

'Ah,' said Heriot, 'you have will-power.'

'Come a long way?'

'It's seemed so.'

'Been out a long time, by the look of you. Them clothes of yours —'

'Yours,' said Heriot, 'aren't elegant either, Sam.'

The old man rattled two pebbles in his hand and rested his head against the wall, staring into the sky. 'Who cares?' he said, half-asleep.

Justin rose and came cautiously towards the shade. He edged up to Heriot. 'Ah, I tired now,' he said, and lay down with his head across Heriot's knees.

Heriot yawned again. And from far away, Sam asked: 'Where you going?'

'God knows.'

'Stock?'

'Here?' said Heriot, smiling. 'No. Two men and one horse.'

'Used to be a bit of stock here one time. No good though. Everything shut down. No one around any more. It was a hell of a long time ago.' His voice faded away into remembering.

'You weren't a missionary?' Heriot said.

'No, not me. Gardener, that was the last thing I was.'

'I was a missionary,' Heriot said.

'What for?' asked Sam, his voice increasingly somnolent. He edged away from Heriot and lay down, his knees up. 'Keep on talking, you'll know when I'm asleep.'

'Expiation,' said Heriot. 'Yes. This is my third life. My third expiation.'

'What was the others?' asked Sam incuriously.

'I suppose it was my birth, as a human being, that drove me to charity. Yes, that was the first. And then there was the massacre, done by my race at Onmalmeri.'

'I heard of it,' said Sam.

'That was the second. It drove me to the mission. And then at the end there was my — my hatred.'

'What'd that drive you to?' murmured Sam.

'That?' said Heriot pensively. 'That has made a lost man of me.'

The old man scratched himself. 'Haven't you ever been happy?' he demanded, with disapproval.

'Happy? Yes, sometimes. But in all my — expiations, there's never been a reconciliation. And what less,' asked Heriot, 'what less could I hope for now?'

A sighing snore came from Sam. Heriot smiled. He lifted Justin's head and moved his knees away.

Three goats followed him as he made his way to the spring. He climbed the fence that enclosed it and stepped through the jungle of cabbage and pumpkin vines towards the brushwood shelter under which the water lay in its cup of built-up stones. He took off his shirt and plunged his torso in the water, and drank deeply, too. But it was warmer than he had hoped, and less refreshing, and he rose spluttering and more tired than before. The sun on his back as he kneeled there seemed to be drawing the blood from his body, and the sick, revolting smell of rotting cabbage was in his nostrils. His stomach moved.

He rose then, shakily, to his feet, and went to the fence, and leaning there vomited, the goats scampering up to watch him. He felt that his body was being torn inside, but at last the retching stopped, he went back with his legs shaking to wash again at the spring.

The two men still lay supine outside the shanty. Pulling on his shirt, Heriot watched the goats nose tentatively round his vomit.

'I am vile,' he told the goats humbly. 'I am vile.'

He climbed the fence and went back to the shack, his legs so weak that he seemed to himself to be fainting as he sank down by Justin, catching the sleeping man's elbow in the crook of his arm.

Screaming, a flock of white cockatoos passed over the shanty and descended on the spring. But their storm of cries could not even suggest a dream to the three sleepers in the shade.

So long, thought Gunn dejectedly, and no sign of them. Is it time to go back? How am I to judge when we should give up?

'Nothing yet,' Rex said. 'Nothing.'

'No.'

'Reckon we'll find him, brother?'

'I don't know. This is a long way to come without seeing a track.'

'Might be they went through gorge, brother.'

'Even if they did, we should have cut their tracks somewhere.'

Stephen said: 'Might be they . . . dead, now.'

'No,' Rex said loudly. 'They not dead.'

'You'd better get used to the idea,' Gunn said. 'Sorry, Rex. But don't count on seeing him again.'

'I got to see him,' Rex said. 'I got to talk to him. We never talk before.'

'It might be too late,' Gunn said. And he was thinking: So would I like to talk to him, clear up some things he wondered about me, whether I'd come back to the mission, for instance. I could tell him now, I could promise him. That'd mean a lot to the old man. So would Rex, much more. So would Stephen. But what chance have we got? Too late now.

Rex stared sullenly ahead. 'You giving up, brother? You not caring about that old man now, eh?'

'That's not true —'

'I never giving up.'

'We must, sometime,' said Gunn. 'Sometime.' Thinking: It's hopeless, already. What's the point of it now? They feel humiliated that he ran away to escape from them, but perhaps they'll get over it, perhaps we'll be able to help them forget it. What's the use of all this stumbling through the wilderness?

The bush man, Naldia, far ahead, stopped, watching the ground, and dismounted, and squatted in the grass, peering.

The sullenness died out of Rex's face and he came alive, kicking his horse forward, shouting to the older man: '*Angundja? Angundja?*'

And Naldia stood up and turned, grinning, proud. ''Ere,' he called, ''ere. Track 'ere.'

10

'And so,' said Heriot, 'there's no way I can help you. I'm reduced to accepting charity at last.'

He looked around the wretched room, taking in the dirt floor, the sagging hessian of the bed, the rusted stove spilling out the old man's only light. On the table lay a cooked haunch of goat, killed in Heriot's honour, and now cold. 'Though your charity's very acceptable,' he said.

'You can't help me,' said Sam. 'I don't want no help. Plenty of people worse off than me. Well, plenty of natives, anyhow.'

'How long,' asked Heriot, 'have you been out?'

'Out? How d'you mean?'

'Out of the world. Civilization. Out of touch, in fact.'

'It'd be two years,' said Sam. 'Yeah, two years ago it was, last time I went down to the town. Hundred and fifty mile it is. I had horses then, but they died on me. Didn't worry me, I was getting too old for it.'

'Yes,' said Heriot. 'We do get old. Quite suddenly.'

'I been here fifteen years. Raising me own tucker and all that. The goats was left here, lot of them gone wild, but I raise up a few. And I got me garden. Don't look too good now,' Sam said apologetically, 'been going off for years. Need some new seed, that's what it is. Same with them scraggy old chickens, but I like the sound of them. Live on nothing at all, they do.'

'You too, Sam,' said Heriot.

'I keep alive,' Sam said. 'God knows why.'

'It's hard to die,' Heriot said.

'You're right there.' The wizened face peered through the firelight, suspicious, curious. 'You're a queer sort of bloke, rolling up like this.'

'I am,' said Heriot, 'a queer sort of bloke.'

'What went wrong with your place?'

'Nothing,' said Heriot, glancing sidelong at him. 'What went wrong here?'

The old man shifted in his chair, sour-mouthed, his eyes full of resentments. 'You know the story,' he said. 'Don't have me on.'

'I don't know it, Sam. Or if I did, I've forgotten.'

'It was — that trouble. Nothing but trouble we ever had with them natives. Didn't like the whitefellow, see, weren't going to take nothing from him — excepting clothes and tucker and tobacco and the like of that, of course. Take any amount of that.'

'I know. We make the best or the worst of them. But why did they hate you?'

'Never had no idea,' Sam said. 'Never could see it myself. Ah, the missionaries, they was a bit hard, maybe — you know, holy, not what you'd call laughing men. And some of the natives went off on stations and come back again hating the white men there. They was too clever, you see, too big for their boots, not right for stations.'

'What were they right for?' Heriot said.

'Couldn't tell you, mate. I know this, but — they wasn't right for here. Just one blow-up after another, all the time I worked here. Then we got the real blow-up that finished it off.'

Tenderly feeling the welt on his shin: 'What was that?' asked Heriot.

The old man looked at him disbelievingly. 'You heard about that, mate. Don't tell me.'

'I can't remember. My memory's not good now.'

'The bomb,' Sam said patiently. 'You know, the bomb the Japs dropped here. Fell in a trench, killed three of the only four white blokes we had here.'

'And that was the end,' said Heriot. 'I remember. But we were busy ourselves then, I suppose I forgot soon after. I remember the planes, of course, and the people running out of the village into the hills, but they didn't bomb us. And there was Broome and Darwin and the *Koolama* to think of.'

From a dark corner: 'I could see their face,' said Justin.

'Whose face?' Sam demanded.

'Them Jap. One time I hiding in the hills and they went over, and I could see these little men looking down out of plane with big goggle on their eyes. I thought I going to die then. I reckon they see, but they just went on, they didn't even bomb me. I real scared that time.'

'Imagine it,' said Heriot dreamily, 'setting out with a load of bombs for a country you'd never seen and wanted to conquer, and when you got there — nothing. Nothing at all for hundreds of miles. And then a few little houses that no one would want to destroy. They must have felt lonely at first.'

'That old man Wandalo,' said Justin, 'he made real good corroboree about when they bombing Broome.'

'Cyclones have done more damage,' Heriot said. '*O imitatores,*' he said scornfully, '*servum pecus.*'

'Voo parlay fronsay,' Sam said. 'Ooay l'estaminay silver play?'

Heriot peered at him through the flickering light. 'You're an old soldier,' he said. Their eyes met and slid away, distrustfully.

'That's right,' said Sam.

'I am, too,' Heriot said. 'I am, too.'

'All right,' said Sam harshly. 'What do you want us to do? Sing songs together?'

112

'No. Anything but that.'

'Took a lot of time to forget those days,' Sam said. 'A lot of time.'

'I know that, Sam.'

'You say it ain't easy to die. It ain't easy to kill, neither.'

'No, harder, much harder.'

'And when you get to want to do it —'

Heriot said sharply: 'Don't say that, Sam.'

He had broken something then. A stillness fell over them, and they were wrapped in memories; Sam, on his chair at the table, head bent over his hands, scrawny profile outlined by firelight; Heriot on the sagging bed, his face turned to the dark floor. Outside, the silence of the moon.

'What are you thinking, Sam?'

The old man licked his lips. 'Thinking we was all animals, that's all. Just animals. No, worse.'

'And suffer more for it. We have pity, and conscience, and reason. Those things hurt.'

'I made a muck of my life,' Sam said.

'That's something animals don't do,' said Heriot.

'Nothing ever turned out right. I never *done* nothing. And these days —'

'You sit and rot,' said Heriot, 'like an old buggy in a shed.'

'What did you do?' asked Sam. 'Anything?'

'I did a little,' Heriot said, 'but what a little when you think what was to be done. Whatever you try to build they knock down with their wars and debates. Sometimes I wonder if there'll ever be a revolt against picking up the pieces.'

Sam turned on his chair, his back to the fire, searching Heriot's face. 'Where you going?' he asked quietly.

'Nowhere,' Heriot said, trying to see the old man's eyes in the shadow. 'Why, Sam?'

'I don't know.'

'Sam —?'

'Yeah?'

'Can I stay with you?' Heriot asked, almost eagerly. 'I could, couldn't I? There's nowhere to go, nothing to do. We could talk, Sam, and wait.'

'Yeah, we could do that.'

'Two old men — it's fitting enough.'

'Time goes slow,' said Sam.

'I want that.'

'You get sick of it — waiting.'

'But there are always new things to think of. Not new to the world, but new to us. Nothing's true until you feel it. That's why we have poets.'

'I don't know,' Sam said. 'Don't know what to say.' He stood up and shuffled across to his stove, his grasshopper-body black against the glow.

'Say what you think,' said Heriot. 'Don't deceive me.'

Sam bent and pushed more wood into the stove, and stood stooped in front of it.

'Be honest, Sam.'

'What would you be doing?' asked Sam privately. And turning back from the fire said, in his cracked voice, 'You'd be mad, mad as I am. What do you think I do here? What's the good of my kind of living? Nothing to live for except eating, and nothing except eating to keep you from dying. And the food hard to come by at that. You'd need to be mad, I tell you.'

'Yes,' said Heriot softly, staring at the fragile body of the old man, the bird-claw hands. 'Yes, you're right.'

'I ain't mean,' Sam insisted. 'I don't mind having you, I'm just thinking of you —'

'I know,' said Heriot gently. He leaned back in deep shadow, hiding his face from the anxious eyes. 'We'll go in the morning, Sam.'

'I must go,' Way said, 'but I thought you two should know about the new men coming and everything. It's cheering news.'

'Yes,' Helen said. 'And you look cheered.'

'More than that,' Dixon said. 'Joyful.'

Way smiled, flushing a little. 'Why shouldn't I? This is a happy day. More staff, more money. Nothing can hold us back now.' He pushed open the screen door and shut himself out. 'Good night,' he called from the darkness. 'God bless us all.'

'Amen,' Helen said. She turned back to Dixon, laughing. 'He really is in a blissful mood. I've never seen him so happy.'

'Well, aren't you?'

'Of course,' she said. 'I could make a speech. This is a great day, a new era is dawning —'

'Scrub it,' he said. 'I don't want to marry a politician. Do you reckon we should have told the padre while he was here?'

'Told him what?'

'About wanting to get hitched.'

'That was the wrong answer,' she said. 'You should have said coyly: "About us." '

'Don't talk smart,' he said. 'I don't want to start beating you before we're married.'

'It's the last chance you'll have, Terry, because Mabel's promised me her fighting stick. What's more, Mabel and the whole village already know about us, and if you don't marry me pretty soon there's going to be some ugly talk.'

'You've got no hope,' he said, laughing, 'of keeping a secret in this place. Arthur asked me this morning if I'd have him for my best man.'

'Ruth wants to be my bridesmaid, too. I promised her.'

'Have I got to marry you with one of those brass rings Father keeps for weddings?'

114

'I won't mind. Brass lasts well.'

He was looking at her, and held out his hand palm upwards on the table, and she put hers in it. 'I feel funny about all this,' he said. 'Doesn't seem like the sort of thing that'd happen to me, somehow.'

'I feel a bit odd, too.'

'Gee, eh, fancy me being married.' He shook his head, looking into her clear eyes, and felt his foreignness leaving him. No need ever again to wander in Darwin, lost as if in a great city, or idle like a gangling waif in Perth or Adelaide. He had his home here, she was his home. Her hand was cool and dry.

She was smiling, intent on him. 'What's funny?' he asked.

'You look like a little boy sometimes,' she said. 'I'll have a little boy like you, running round naked with the other children.'

'Ah,' he said, embarrassed, 'have as many as you like.'

'Everyone's so happy now,' she said. 'Not only us. If only Bob and Rex and Stephen were back —'

He dropped his eyes, his hand slackening. 'Listen —' he said. 'What about Bob?'

'Bob doesn't want anyone,' she said gently. 'Not yet. He's a lonely man, like Mr Heriot. Don't think about Bob, Terry. You'd be wrong.'

'Would I?' he said, looking up again. 'That's good. I wanted to be honest. . . .'

He put out his other hand and she took it. 'You are honest,' she said, and because he was poor in words they sat silent, and looked at one another across the table.

In the early morning they crossed the little plain and came once again into the hills. Pigeons with delicate antennae scattered from the rocks, but Heriot no longer noticed such things, deeply weary as he was, and sick, and full of valedictions. The country before him was an endless recurrence of rock and grass and tree; all that could be seen had been seen, all that could be learned would never be learned, never now. He sat like wood in the saddle and loved nothing but the constant sky.

Before nightfall they crossed and camped at a small freshwater river in a valley filled with tall gumtrees and cadjiputs, and dense ferns and pandanus and tropic shrubs draped with wild passion-fruit vines and the laced and furred white flowers of the wild cucumber. Clear water ran shallowly over the stones and in the broad pools appeared the fleeting shadows of fish. It was a calm and gentle place, yet Heriot slept brokenly, and woke in the morning surprised by the sun. For death was his one thought and destination, and he saw himself now as a minute lizard in the grass, over which death hovered and hung like a hawk, delaying the strike out of delight in its own power.

Climbing the hills again in the morning he shivered, and cried out to Justin for reassurance. 'We're very small,' he said.

'You big bloke, brother,' Justin said kindly.

'No, no, you don't understand. Think of it. This world. A little molten pebble spinning in air. This rock we walk on, a thin skin, changing every second. And the trees, what are they?'

'They just trees, brother.'

'A little fur, less than the bloom on a peach. But we creep under them. And in the split seconds between the heaving of the earth millions of generations of us are born and grow and die.'

'Might be, brother,' Justin allowed.

'I'm a philosopher,' said Heriot, in self-derision. 'I'll be silent now.'

And indeed he was silent almost all that day, and though they camped once again without water, and nausea welled up in him as he chewed the chunks of cold, cooked goat that Sam had given them, he had no complaint or comment. But he slept uneasily, tormented by the cries of dingoes, and on the next day he was weaker, and more tremulous of the hands.

'I'll walk now,' he said. 'I've had enough riding.'

'No,' said Justin, 'you stay on horse, brother. You tired.'

'I'll walk,' said Heriot firmly.

But at midday, in the full heat of the sun, he stumbled among the rocks, and fell, and was unable to rise.

Justin, kneeling over him, sweating into his beard, pleaded: 'Brother, brother, don't you lie there. Get up now, brother.'

'I can't,' Heriot said. 'Not again. No, Justin, leave me here.'

'You got to get up. There no water here, nothing. Come away, brother.'

'There's no help for it,' said Heriot. 'Leave me.' The rocks burned him through his clothes and he closed his eyes. The sun glowed and then darkened through his lids, and he felt sleep coming.

But Justin, stooping, lifted the old man in his arms, and set him on his feet and supported him. There was not now any urgency in Justin, only a hopeless calm. 'We go on,' he said flatly. 'I get you up on the horse and you sit there and I look after you.'

'No,' said Heriot feebly. 'No.'

But he was bundled, unresisting, into the saddle, and sat limp and tired while the world passed in a blur of sunlight, and the sweat streamed from his back, and his tongue grew dry as canegrass with thirst, making it hard to speak. Yet he muttered to himself from time to time. 'Why try to save me?' he demanded. 'Who cares? This world — this world's a grain of salt. A grain of salt in an ocean. No microscope is strong enough to see me. No camera is fast enough to catch me between birth and dying.'

He looked down at the tangled hair of Justin and felt pity for him. 'This earth hates us,' he said gently. 'It heaves and strains under our feet. Go home, Justin. You haven't had your share of time.'

'No,' said Justin. 'I not leaving you.'

'The world wants us to prey. But I won't prey on you, no, I'll go against the world. Soon I won't prey on anything. Not even the insects this horse crushes carrying me.'

'That right, brother.'

Heriot shook his head, gasping in his dry throat. 'Why do we have thirst? Because the world hates us.'

'Might be.'

'And hunger? Oh, God. Suppose you had an open wound. The maggots would be in it now, eating you up. That's hunger.'

'Yes,' said Justin. 'Yes.'

'There's some wasp that lays its eggs inside caterpillars. The grubs eat the caterpillar, but it doesn't die. No, they keep it alive so that they can eat it longer.'

'Yes,' said Justin.

'They keep it alive until it makes its cocoon. Then they finish eating it, they use the cocoon themselves. That's hunger,' said Heriot, 'that's what I mean by preying.'

'Yes, brother.'

'But I'll escape it,' Heriot vowed. 'I won't be party to it. No. Now I'm only the prey.'

And then he was silent again, choked by thirst, and sat and swayed in the saddle as brown man and brown horse plodded on over the hot rock. His smallness and his futility could not hurt him now, for he had no pride, had nothing, only his feeble body, and his thirst.

He was almost asleep when they came, after hours, to the country of caves, where bluffs and cliffs of rock were split with dark holes, and where, green and luxuriant, a *gle* tree reached out from among the boulders.

'There water there,' Justin said, on a long sigh. 'Water, brother.'

'Ah, *benigna natura*,' said Heriot wryly.

They paused for a moment to rest their eyes on the dark foliage, so fresh among so much rock; and as they stood there, a small sound came from among the leaves, and Justin, stepping back, reached for the rifle, and loaded stealthily, and began to creep forward.

On a shelf of rock a wallaby sat, so soft in its grey fur that it might have been a toy, so innocent, with its big foolish ears and dark eyes, that nothing in all its life could have threatened it, thought Heriot, feeling with his eyes the tranquil heart beating in the side and the claws gripping stone. 'Oh, my beauty,' he said softly, 'my handsome one.' And the wallaby, turning its head towards him, started. And Justin fired. The perfect creature leaped and fell back, and died quivering on the flat rock.

Heriot closed his eyes.

'Come here, brother,' Justin shouted. But he shook his head and said nothing.

'Water,' Justin said. 'Plenty here. Quick, brother.'

He moved wearily in the saddle, stirring the horse forward and allowing it to carry him on to the little rock pond beneath the wild fig tree.

There was grass growing in the water, and a continual slow drip from the overhanging cliff far above. A drop fell stingingly on the back of his neck as he lay down over the rocks to drink.

Long afterwards he got to his feet again and walked towards the mouth of the cave close by the pond. And under hanging rock he saw the first of the paintings, the crude figure of a man without a mouth, his head outlined with a horseshoe shape like that of the rainbow serpent.

'I know you,' he said. 'You are Wolaro. God. What does it matter what you're named?'

He called to Justin: 'Look, here is God.' But when he turned towards Justin, the man's eyes were wide and frightened, his lips were dry and he licked them.

'Why,' said Heriot, 'you're not afraid? Justin —'

Justin said hoarsely: 'Brother — brother, don't you go in there. Come back, brother.'

'This is my house now,' said Heriot. 'Don't be afraid.'

He stepped into the cave, and from all the walls the mouthless god looked down on him.

'Hail,' he said. '*Ali.*'

He moved, and something rolled from his feet. It was a skull. The floor of the cave was littered with human bones.

He was very tired. He lay down against the cave-wall and closed his eyes, quiet and cool. 'I have come home now,' he said. 'This is home.'

11

Long afterwards Justin overcame his fear a little and came into the cave. But there was terror still in his eyes, and he, who more than any of his people had denied the old beliefs, had at last to acknowledge the powers of the dark upon his blood, and the strength of the dead.

The light of their fire washed the rough walls, illuminating the staring god, dancing in the sockets of the staring skulls. They could feel no hunger there, though the meat of the wallaby burned sweetly on the coals. Crouching close by Heriot, Justin piled on the fire more of the wood he had dragged in to keep back the darkness; and all night lay sleepless and afraid, the spirits haunting in and out of his brain.

'What will become of me?' asked Heriot, deeply and softly in shadow. 'Where will I go, Justin?'

The brown man stirred beside him. 'How you mean, brother?'

'This is the end. You know that. And when I'm dead, what then?'

'Don't say that.'

'But I must now, there's need for it. Justin,' said Heriot rebelliously, 'I don't want to die. No. Now why is that?'

'You won't die, brother, not now.' But the man was struggling, and his voice showed it, against Heriot's conviction. 'Go sleep, brother.'

'Will my spirit go back and wait to be born? I'd like that. Wait at Onmalmeri, in the water deep under the lilies, and when some woman came, enter her body and be a child again. Would that happen, Justin?'

'No,' said Justin sadly. 'That don't happen.'

'Where will I go, then? Only to the islands? And wait there forever, and be nothing? And never,' asked Heriot, pleading, 'never come again?'

'No,' said Justin, 'you never come again. Never, brother.' He was touched with grief.

'What will you do with me? Put me high in a tree, and when I'm dry carry my bones away?'

'No,' Justin protested, 'I bury you under cross and say prayer for you, and you go right to heaven, brother.'

'*Alunggur njarianangga,*' prayed Heriot. '*Arung ada bram. Manambara balngi* —'

'Thy Kingdom come. Thy will be done. On earth, as it is in heaven —'

'That's hell where His will is done as on earth.'

'Don't say that, brother.'

'What reason not to say it now? Justin — I want my bones to be buried at Onmalmeri. Or left here. Yes, here will do, this old burying ground.'

'Please,' Justin begged, 'please, go sleep now.'

'My spirit can come back, for a little time. Can't it? I can visit someone I love?'

'They say —' said Justin. 'They say spirit come back to his brother, if he a man, or to his wife. Or might be hang around the bush and come if someone say his name.'

'But you don't believe that. You say dead people's names, you're the only one who does. You don't believe in spirits.'

The light flickering over his face, with its dark lines running across the forehead and from nostril to mouth: 'Yes,' Justin said, 'I believe.'

'After so long —'

'My old man was real clever old man. He could send his spirit from mission to town, brother, and sit in tree like a bird, and talk to the people there. They didn't see him, but they heard him all right, talking to them.'

'Say my name, Justin. When I'm dead, go out some night in the dark and say my name.'

'One time his spirit bring tobacco for my brother from the town. Might be you don't believe that —'

'Promise you'll say my name.'

'I can't say you name,' Justin said. 'And I don't know all you name.'

'My name is Stephen.'

'Stephen,' said Justin. 'Real nice name, that.'

'Call me that. Say: "I'll call your name, Stephen." '

Hesitating unhappily: 'I can't say that, brother,' said Justin. 'It don't sound right.'

'No,' said Heriot wistfully. 'After so long — but we're always foreign. That never ends.'

The fire leaped in his regarding eyes. 'I'm not so small as I was. No, I'm growing now. There are powers in me. I have love, and courage, a little of it, and reason of a sort, and compassion. And I'm a very beautiful machine, Justin, and so are you, although we're so fragile. And if I'm going to die — well, my life has been pretty long by the standards of moths. Why, if I were as big as a tree and lived as long, I'd be proud, sinfully proud. But I'm not proud now, not with the eyes of all these skulls on me. . . .'

'Brother — Stephen —' pleaded Justin. 'You go sleep now.'

'In the morning you must go,' said Heriot.

'I not going. Not yet.'

'Think of Ella, Justin.'

'I been thinking of her. And my little kids. Ah, my little kids,' said Justin, 'they be real glad when their daddy come home.'

'Then go,' said Heriot violently. 'Why have you come so far with me when your children need you? That was selfish of you. Of you, not of me.'

'You need me, brother — Stephen.'

'I don't need you now. Why, man, do you think I want you standing round when I'm dying? Go, tomorrow.'

His skin shining in the red light, the brown man turned his face away from the eyes of Heriot, and from the eyes of the painted god and from the holes of the skulls. He hid from them, pulling up the blanket over his tangled hair.

'I going,' he said, 'Stephen.'

When Heriot woke Justin was gone, and he felt a sudden panic at the thought that there would be no chance to say farewell to him and thank him and send back messages with him to the world. But when he came out of the cave-mouth Justin was below, squatting by the water, and at the sight of the familiar profile, the heavy, wrinkled brow, flattened nose and black beard, Heriot sighed.

'Justin,' he said, 'don't go — don't go without telling me.'

The dark man rose and came towards the cave, his face earnest and sad. 'I don't go yet,' he said.

'It would be futile, wouldn't it, to try to tell you how much your companionship has meant to me. And how deeply it's touched me to think that I — had a hand in turning out a man like you.'

'You don't have to say nothing.'

'No. Because you know everything now, don't you. We've become — close enough.'

'I never forget you.'

'Nor will I forget you,' said Heriot. And they held each other by the eyes, words being of no use to them at the time of farewells.

'There's something,' Heriot said, 'something I wanted to tell you. Look after Stephen. Watch him, Justin. Teach him. Make him like you. He's a good boy, I want him to be like you.'

'I do that,' Justin said. 'I watch him.'

'And there's something more,' said Heriot, fumbling in his pockets. 'There's Rex. I'll give you these things, you see, my knife and this watch. There's not much, but take them, and say they're for Rex, and the rifle, too. I know you'd like them, and you've earned them, and you'll have them, too, but say they're for Rex.'

'I say that all right,' Justin promised. 'But why you doing this?'

'I want them to know I didn't hate him. I didn't, Justin. It was because I loved him — loved all your people — that I did — that thing I did. They'll understand that. They'll know there was never one of them I hated. They'll remember, some of them, loving a woman and finding she was no good and wanting to kill her. And if they realized then it was love, not hate, that drove them, they'll understand me and forgive me. Tell them all of that.'

'I tell them,' Justin said softly.

'It's my only defence. It's the world's only defence, that we hurt out of love, not out of hate.'

'Yes, brother.'

'It's a feeble defence,' said Heriot, with sadness, 'and a poor reconciliation. But we've nothing better.'

'No.'

'Well — you must go, Justin.'

The brown man turned his face towards Heriot, and his mouth was stiff with grief. 'I can't do that,' he said. 'I can't leave you.'

'No,' said Heriot, 'don't say that again. Think of Ella and the children. You'd be doing me wrong if you made me responsible for taking you from them.'

'Leave you here, all hungry, and let you die?'

'Hush,' said Heriot. 'You have the rifle.'

'Yes, it down there.'

'And how many bullets?'

'Just one,' said Justin, with an unhappy laugh, 'just one little fella.'

'I'm sorry. But you'll find something. There's always been something to kill.'

'Yes. Yes.'

'Go now.'

'You go inside,' Justin said, 'just a minute, brother. Please.'

'Why?' asked Heriot.

But the man's eyes pleaded with him, and he went into the cave and waited. And when the shot came, he knew why it was, and he groaned in his throat. A long time afterwards he came out again, knowing he would find the horse well dead and past all pain.

Justin was hacking at the carcass with Heriot's knife, his face tense and still.

'You loved that horse,' Heriot said.

'I don't know.'

'This is the last death I'll cause. The last, I promise you.'

'I know that, brother.'

'I didn't want food. There was nothing I wanted now.'

'You got to eat.'

'No, I don't, now. That's the beauty of it.'

'Hush,' said Justin, 'you be quiet now.' He came up to the cave with chunks of meat in his hands and laid them on a ledge inside. 'Everything ready now, brother.'

'Stephen.'

'Stephen.'

Slowly Heriot stretched out his hands and laid them on Justin's chest. 'This is how to say good-bye,' he said, 'among your people.'

'I can't touch you, Stephen. My hands all bloody.'

'All our hands are bloody,' said Heriot bitterly. 'Say good-bye.'

Then Justin laid his hands lightly on the old man's breast, and they looked at one another, dark sunken eyes into strained blue ones. The air was full of farewells, but they stood in silence.

'Ah, Justin,' said Heriot, turning away, 'you're my good deeds, my salvation from myself. . . .

'I never forget you, Stephen.'

'Look after your children, for my sake.'

'I do that, always.'

'You must go.'

'Yes,' said Justin. 'I go now.' He walked away past the pool, stooping to pick up his spears and the rifle, and vanished finally behind an outcrop of rock. A little wind stirred sadly in the leaves of the *gle* tree; and Heriot, at the mouth of his cave, turned, and hid his face against the body of the painted god.

In the dimness of the cave, days ran together and lost themselves, so that Heriot, sleeping, eating, or disjointedly thinking, felt time confounded, a twilight without divisions, and himself a simple plant of the sea's floor, waving and dying.

He had thought there would be much to think about in this last solitude, but his mind was placid and empty. Justin faded in memory even on the first day, and on the second the features of his face became impossible to recall. Only faces of the past, Margaret's face, and Esther's, drifted now and then across the screen of his eyelids.

And on the third day, late in the afternoon, with the flies humming drowsily around the rank meat, the cave became at last insupportable to him. He got slowly to his feet and went out into the failing light.

There was nausea in his stomach, and his legs shook. But he made his way carefully over the rocks to the nearest hill, and then down, and on again. The light grew fainter, but the moon rose early and was close to full, and he went on.

Far away a dingo cried out. But he was not afraid.

But after hours, it seemed, of this clambering and stumbling his weakness struck him down, and he lay among the rocks and with one hand hid his eyes from the yellow moon. His hair was whiter than moonlight, and his face dark. The dingo howled again, but he was too feeble to build a fire, and had no fear.

Over his head a stunted tree waved, its leaves outlined with silver light. He thought he had never seen anything so beautiful, and could have lain and stared at it all night; but his eyes clouded and he dropped suddenly into a black sleep.

Long and thin up the gully: '*Bau!*' shouted a voice. And the riders on the hillside halted and turned, searching the rocks, the bushes.

The cry came again.

'Ah,' said Rex, deep in his throat. He turned his horse down a hillside and rode from his companions; who, watching him recede down the gully, became aware also of a dark, moving figure, a tired man urging himself on through the boulders.

It was the end, Gunn knew; and he had not expected this sense of bereavement which descended on him so belatedly.

Now the two figures were close, and Rex had dismounted; but Justin had stopped, his face turned to the other man, and would not approach him. It was left to Rex to advance over the last few yards between them, and even when they were face to face Justin would make no movement, but stood stooped and frozen, his eyes intent.

Then Rex reached out and touched his shoulder. And slowly the older man's hand went to his pocket, and he brought it out again and laid it in Rex's, and held out the rifle for Rex to take. Yet there was still a strange dream quality in their movements, neither moving his eyes by a fraction from the other's. Until Rex, gently and humbly, bent his head and touched Justin's shoulder with his forehead; and the other man's hand appeared and lay lightly across his back.

On the hillside, sweating in the heat: 'This is all,' Gunn said softly. 'You can go home now, Stephen.'

Stephen, his eyes fixed on the two dwarfs in the valley, nodded, his mouth taut and sad.

'Hard to believe it's over,' Gunn said. 'Hard to believe. Nothing will be the same again.'

High on the hill, overlooking the reconciliation of Heriot, his foster-father, Stephen bent his head. 'No,' he said quietly. 'Nothing going to be the same,' he promised.

The old man's eyes came slowly open, and he saw the sun sitting half below the next rise. He was hot and choked with thirst, could not remember when the rocks had exuded such heat or when he had sweated so. It was intolerable. He rose shakily to his feet and stepped forward towards the sunrise. The hill grew tall in front of him, reaching up to hide the sun.

'Who am I?' he asked, dazed, half-blinded. 'My name was Heriot. A son of the sun.'

He began to sing, in the midst of his stumbling, a wild corroboree song about himself.

> 'Ali! Bungundja bugurga, nandaba brambun?
> Worai! Heriot ngarang, nawuru morong nangga.'

And he asked: 'Where are you going, old ghost? Going to the islands, are you? Going to Bundalmeri? He is your lord. His country is outside — outside.'

124

> '*Worai! mudumudu-gu ngarambun,*
> *Gre-gu Bundalmeri nangga.*
> *Bungama ngaia, beni brara.*
> *Walawa gre beninangga,*
> *Walawa ada bram.*
> *Worai! Worai!*'

An eaglehawk hung over him, great ragged wings curved around air. '*Worai!*' said Heriot. 'Alas. The earth's hungry.'

He was staggering then to the top of a rocky rise, and when he came there he stood suddenly still, his white hair blowing against the sky, his eyes dazzled with the sea.

It was the sea's shine, and the sea's noise, shattered against rock cliffs. Ultimate indeed, at last found. And the sun that had led him hung close over the sea, not rising but setting, not lighting but blinding.

He came forward to the edge of the cliffs, where they dropped, vast red walls, to the faraway sea below. And the sea, where the light was not on it, was the blue-green of opals and endlessly rearing, smashed into white at the foot of the rock.

There was a break in the cliffs, and he climbed unsteadily down a few yards to a red ledge with a shallow cave behind it. The skulls were there again, and the eyes of the mouthless god, turned forever towards the islands. But the islands — the islands. He stared out to sea and saw nothing but the sun on the water; his dreams and his fears all true, and there were no islands.

He turned, blinded, away, and saw on the ledge beside him a block of stone fallen from the cliff. And he stooped, straining, and lifted it in his arms. He knew suddenly the momentousness of his strength, his power to alter the world at will, to give to the sea what the sea through an eternity of destruction was working to engulf, this broken rock. Truly, he would work a change on the world before it blinded him.

Poised on the ledge, he threw the stone, and it floated slowly, slowly down the huge cliff face, and crashed against it; and slower and slower entered the sea, in a tiny circle of spray.

And watching it, he staggered, and stepped back towards the cave, shaking in the legs, and in his head following the enormous fall into the waves.

High overhead the eagle patrolled the cliff. But suddenly, passing under it, a gull flew out from the rock and planed towards the sun until it was hidden in light. And when the sun sank lower, there, in the heart of the blaze, might appear the islands.

The old man kneeled among the bones and stared into the light. His carved lips were firm in the white beard, his hands were steady, his ancient blue eyes, neither hoping nor fearing, searched sun and sea for the least dark hint of a landfall.

'My soul,' he whispered, over the sea-surge, 'my soul is a strange country.'